D1526354

ALSO BY SONORA TAYLOR

SOMEONE TO SHARE MY NIGHTMARES: STORIES

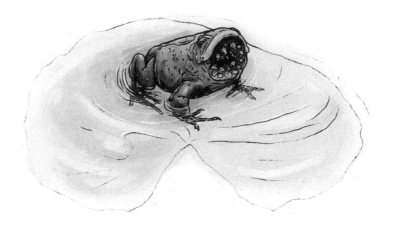

BY SONORA TAYLOR

Someone to Share My Nightmares: Stories by Sonora Taylor

Cover art by Doug Puller.

TABLE OF CONTENTS

A list of content and trigger warnings can be found at the back of this book, before About the Author.

To Will, my dearest love.

FOREWORD

Sonora Taylor is someone I consider a dear friend, and happens to be my fellow co-founder of Fright Girl Summer (frightgirlsummer.com). When I was going through a difficult time, she sent me a care package full of witchy gifts. It was exactly what I needed at the moment. She genuinely cares for people. I'm proud to call Sonora my horror sister even though we have never met in person. You can find her on social media advocating for writers from marginalized communities or sharing her collection of the BEST earrings.

Besides being a wonderful human, she is a splendid voice in horror right now. And this is most definitely a time when women are leaving their mark in horror. We are redefining what it is and how it is told. From the horrors we experience with our bodies, life experiences, love and the mundane, there is a huge shift in the genre. Women are charging through fearlessly not caring if they are called shrill or crazy.

Sonora's work reflects the shift happening below our feet. She is not only part of the shift, but she is also cheering on other women in the game. She was one of the first people to read and review my work. Knowing you have support in what can be a difficult journey makes the road less arduous. That is the reason we began Fright Girl Summer. It's my absolute honor to sit here and sing Sonora's praises. However, when you read her books it doesn't take long to know the work speaks for itself.

The title of this collection says it all. *Someone To Share My Nightmares* is horror with a caress of the sensual. It's a seamless silk stocking held up by lace, and what you don't see is the blade tucked beneath the thigh. I absolutely love sex written into horror by women. The combination is a pointed edge pressed into your mind and flesh with just enough pressure to stimulate, but not hurt.

Our experiences in love and sex can sometimes be described as horror. Can Krampus be hot? Yes, he can, and I could hear his voice ooze with desire in the final story, "'Tis Better To Want." It fulfilled all my secret fantasies from the 1985 film *Legend*. I could see the larger-than-life creature waiting for me in his bedchamber. *sigh*

Another fantastic aspect to Sonora's short stories are the endings. They always leave you satisfied, yet titillated, or with a chill running down your back. Sex or romantic elements in horror don't mean it cannot also be scary or haunting. I believe this thinking has been engrained because horror has largely been dominated by men. Not that men can't write sex or romance, but women have their own unique experiences that must be heard. Sonora gives us a brilliant example that you do not have to sacrifice the very natural act of sex to create a creepy story. The horror elements still come through.

Sonora also takes the opportunity to show that sexuality is fluid. The boundaries when it comes to love and sex do not have to conform to any set rules. This is true of this collection and her novel, *Without Condition*. "Bump in The Night" is a cheeky story of fluid sexuality reminiscent of the 2009 film *Drag Me to Hell*. But arousing! It is written better than I can describe it.

"The Sharps" is probably one of my favorites in the collection because it is a mix of sci-fi, horror, and romance. It's imaginative with a delicious degree of tension. "Candy" had me howling because there are always snippets of humor in Sonora's writing. Your emotions are given a ride as you move thought this collection and that is what keeps you turning the page. How will she surprise me next?

Fans of Sonora's previous work will enjoy this collection. If you are new to Sonora, please pick up a copy of *Seeing Things* and *Without Condition*. Both are two very different stories of women experiencing horror in their day to day lives. One is grounded in the supernatural and the other could be true. It doesn't take long for you to become fully invested in their tales.

Share her work and be sure to leave reviews when you can. It all helps women in horror continue to make strides in genre fiction. And is there anything better than discovering a new voice?

V. Castro

SOMEONE TO SHARE MY NIGHTMARES

Kristin's favorite director was in town. He'd been there for almost a month, buried in a grassy knoll at the top of the local cemetery. His stone was the largest, a beacon whose notebooks, flowers, statues, and other items left in tribute cast a gilded shadow on the graves that were unknown to all except their families and friends left behind.

Jonathan Ransom had not been born in Kristin's town. He hadn't even lived there. But he made sure he'd stay there in death, buried in Thornhill Cemetery in the small town of Creekwood, North Carolina.

Ransom's films were haunting portraits of the South, bringing forth that unsettled quiet that most Southerners only knew as a feeling or a sense of innate displeasure with one's surroundings—a quiet anger they couldn't quite place. Ransom manifested that anger into ghosts, shadows, and monsters. He formed them into shapes, created characters that explained Kristin's deepest suspicions about where she lived. His work was celebrated across the country, and his last three films had each garnered more praise than the next.

Ransom claimed that in Creekwood, he'd found his muse. Its empty trees, barren even in summer, and blackened creeks that flowed inches deep brought a mood to his films that actors never could. Kristin knew those scenes well, had known them ever since she first entered the woods that Ransom found delightful. She always tried to see him shoot. He was famous for only shooting at dusk or at dawn, and in the quietest corners of Creekwood that even the locals managed to avoid.

If she'd had the chance to meet him, she would've been able to tell him to avoid those corners.

Ransom's death was called an accident. A local found him at the bottom of a ditch, and his head was bent in an unnatural angle against the stone. Ransom's camera lay shattered next to him, all the film exposed and ruined. No one would see what Ransom saw ever again.

Kristin always knew there was something wrong with the woods outside of her house. Its trees bent at odd shapes, and they never seemed to bear blossoms or fruit. Yet they lived, year in and year out. Birds built nests in their crevices, squirrels burrowed in their holes. Eggs fell to the ground before they hatched, and hawks left the bloodied remains of the squirrels on the roots.

The forest's horrors began to appear in her dreams as early as elementary school. Kristin would fall asleep and in her mind, she'd wander into a forest that no longer hid behind the trappings of flora and fauna. Between craggy trees stood corpses, their mouths frozen into a scream as their arms and hands stretched to the sky alongside the branches. The leaves on the forest floor were strewn with hair and teeth. Each nightmare ended with smoke curling at Kristin's feet and the glow of two eyes blinking in front of her. When she awoke in the safety of her room, she'd vow to stay away from such a dangerous place.

And yet, Kristin couldn't stay away. She'd walk by the woods and feel as if the smoke in her dreams were nipping at her ankles like a wolf puppy, welcoming her into its wild domain. And when she entered the woods, she felt an eerie sense of calm, like whatever had beckoned her was grateful for the company. She knew when she was welcome, and when she should leave. It was as if the demon the eyes in her nightmares belonged to allowed her in so long as she listened to their whispers and left when they told her.

All of his fans mourned his passing, but Kristin also mourned the loss of someone else—perhaps the only some-one—who understood those woods the way she had. When Jonathan Ransom spoke of the forests of Creekwood, it had been like listening to her own thoughts made clear. Whenever she'd shared them with anyone, they called her ridiculous or, at best, said she had the potential to write horror. Jonathan Ransom wrote horror, but what made his horror so compel-ling was his belief in it being real. Not a belief in monsters or ghosts, but a belief in something sinister, something made manifest in the limited ways people could see it. Kristin saw it in her nightmares. Ransom gave her nightmares life.

Kristin knew, deep down, that the woods were the woods. She wouldn't give in to the seductive pull of the nightmare of the forest until she told herself emphatically that it was a nightmare, a fantasy she enjoyed the same as any horror film. It was her imagination—one that, until Jonathan Ransom took up residence beneath the grassy knoll at the end of Thornhill Cemetery, she thought she'd shared with someone else.

But Kristin wasn't going to the cemetery today. She was going straight to the source of her current pain: the ditch that had taken Jonathan Ransom's life. She walked through the silent woods, quiet even though it was still the afternoon. She carried a rose to leave at the ditch.

As she neared the site of Ransom's death, the silence slowly began to slip away. She thought she heard a rustling, but as she got closer, it became a trickle. There were no creeks in the forest, at least not close to here.

Kristin entered the clearing where the ditch had once been. In its place was a creek. The stone that broke Jonathan Ransom's neck was now covered by rushing water.

Kristin sighed. The rainstorms from the previous week must have left their remnants in the woods. Or else the woods wanted to wash him away from her memory for good.

She tossed the rose in the water, then walked away. She'd had enough of the forest for one afternoon.

———

"I see demons every day. I want others to see them too."

Jonathan Ransom's eyes pierced through the lens as he spoke. His voice trembled from Kristin's phone and settled in her ears as she sat in her car. He spoke calmly of the things that scared most everyone else.

"I want others to see what I see," he continued as he spoke with Chelsea Davenport in a rare interview. It was three years old, between his first Oscar and his last completed film. "And I don't want them to deny that they saw it. That's why I lay demons bare in imagery that exists without special effects.

Tree branches, shadows, a dark creek. All contain demons, and film helps me show those demons in ways that others can't avoid."

"So you believe in demons?" Chelsea asked off-camera. The camera wouldn't dare leave Ransom's face. He was so stoic, so calm about fear. The camera wanted to confront viewers with Ransom's calmness. It was more unsettling than any demon he spoke of.

"Yes," he replied, as if Chelsea had asked if the sky were blue or if chocolate was delicious. "But not in the way you're thinking."

"What way am I thinking?"

"The way everyone does: silly monsters summoned from Hell. Candles, the wrong incantation, fire. Horns and cloven feet. Blood and fangs, tits and cocks in wretched proportions." His smile grew. "Did I embarrass you, Ms. Davenport?"

"We don't really talk about tits and cocks on network TV."

"Then you shouldn't be speaking to me about monsters." He chuckled, then continued, "But I don't believe in those demons. Those are the demons everyone believes in, the ones they make up so they can pretend that evil isn't human. That it isn't a part of the world, a chaos as inherent to living as oxygen. It's all a part of life. Evil, like goodness, is very much human; and all we can do when we see it is try to stop it."

"Or in your case, film it."

"I film it in an effort to stop it. I was drawn to film because film magnifies life in ways that help us see what we miss every day. I wanted to magnify the demons so that people would see them more easily."

"You seem to be frightening them, if reviews of your last film are any indication."

Ransom smiled. It cast a pleasant chill on Kristin's heart, like a breeze breaking through the August humidity.

"Isn't fear what compels us all?" Ransom asked.

The YouTube clip stopped, and part two of the interview was about to begin. Kristin stopped the video and put her phone away, then looked out across the field toward the woods.

Water running over where Ransom had died had bothered her more than it should. It almost seemed like the woods delighted in Ransom's death and had seen his flesh as a means of creation. Kristin knew it was silly to think so, and yet she couldn't shake the feeling. Something was wrong with the forest. She'd seen it, and Ransom had seen it too. Had the woods wanted to stop him from seeing it?

She narrowed her eyes at the trees as the late afternoon sun glowed overtop of them. The light was purely August, golden and fat with excess heat. The tree branches stretched toward the sky, begging for rain; and yet they stood proud, knowing that nothing and no one could expose them. Not even a director who'd seen them for what they were.

Kristin saw the woods for what they were. Would the forest do something to her?

She turned off her car and got out. These were crazy thoughts. She needed something to dull those thoughts, and the small bar on the side of the loneliest road in Creekwood would be just the ticket.

————

Kristin stirred the cherry in her drink. The ice had already begun to melt, rendering her Jack and ginger more watery than a high schooler's eyes when their favorite character died on the CW. Condensation covered the glass and slicked her palms. The only thing more useless than her visit to Jonathan Ransom's death site that day was trying to have a cold drink in a Carolina summer.

"Want me to freshen you up there?"

Kristin looked up and saw Evangeline, the bartender, smiling at her. Kristin managed a weak smile back, then gulped her drink down in three swallows. "Yes please," she said as she set down her glass towards Evangeline's end of the bar.

She grabbed a clean glass and filled it with ice. Jack Daniel's and ginger ale followed, along with another cherry. A line of condensation formed almost as soon as Kristin took the glass.

"You'd never know we fixed the air conditioner last week," Evangeline said.

"You sure it's working?" Doug called from his seat. He was a barfly Kristin was convinced slept in the corner booth.

"Sure it's working, it's just hot." Regardless, Evangeline waved her hand in front of the lone air conditioning vent over the bar. Kristin sipped her drink and wondered how long it would take to not only forget her wasted afternoon, but the useless conversation happening next to her.

"Excuse me."

Kristin looked up at the unfamiliar voice. Her eyes widened, and she was glad that the man standing in the doorway was facing Evangeline and not her. He was so handsome that Kristin didn't think he could possibly be real. Every feature, from his sandy blond hair to his strong chin, from his dark eyes to his broad shoulders, seemed crafted to elicit lust in anyone who looked at him.

Anyone, maybe, except Evangeline. "Yes?" she asked, with about the same level of interest she'd show any stranger walking into her bar.

"Do you sell food? I've been wandering around all day and I'm starving."

The man was barely sweating. Had he done a glam-up in his car before coming in?

Evangeline smiled and tossed a small bag of potato chips onto the bar. "This is about it," she said. "But you can order delivery here if you want."

"Will do." The man moved towards the bar, and Kristin noticed how close the potato chips were to her seat. She glanced at Evangeline, who winked at her before turning back to the bar to get a refill of Doug's favorite beer.

"This seat taken?" the man asked with a smile as he moved to sit down.

"No. Go ahead." Kristin took a large sip of her drink to try and calm her eyes back into a normal width.

"Thanks." He pulled the chips toward him and immediately became immersed in his phone. Kristin shrugged to herself and turned back to the bar.

"You have any recommendations?" the man asked.

Kristin turned and saw him looking at her. "Recommendations?"

"For food. You live around here?"

"Oh. Yeah, I'm local." Was it that obvious? Her fingers flicked to her hair to straighten it. She stopped herself, then realized her fingers were floating by her cheek. She curled them under her cheek, then her chin. She hoped she didn't look like as much of a spaz as she felt.

The man smiled, and Kristin felt everything in her body calm except for her heart, which beat so hard she could feel it pulse between her thighs. "So what do you recommend?" he asked.

"Mike's," Kristin replied. "Mike's Deli. They deliver and they make a great turkey club."

"Perfect." The man turned away from her and tapped in his order. Kristin's shoulders fell a little, but when she turned back, she saw a refreshed Jack and ginger in front of her.

"And what'll you have with that club sandwich?" Evangeline asked the man. Kristin kept her eyes away from him.

"I'll have whatever she's having," he answered. Kristin glanced at him, and saw him smiling at her. "Seems like she has good taste."

Evangeline gave Kristin a sly look, one Kristin hoped the man didn't notice. "She does," she said as she made the man's drink.

"I have good taste too!" Doug called.

"You like whatever's on draft!" Evangeline shot back.

"Whatever's on draft is good!"

"So good you spend the rest of the time complaining about my AC, my lights, the smell—"

"It smells too clean in here! You need cigarette smoke or something!"

"I'll light up your ass if you don't shut up!" Evangeline thunked the man's drink in front of him, then grabbed herself a bottle of beer and walked to Doug's table.

"Seems like a fun place to drink," the man said.

"It's something," Kristin said as she turned to face him.

"Well, here's to new places." He held up his drink. "And new friends, I hope."

Kristin smiled back and clinked her glass to his. "Cheers." They took their sips, and Kristin added, "Though friends know each other's names."

The man chuckled. "That they do." He held out his hand. "I'm Joshua."

"Kristin." She shook his hand, and even through the cold water left behind from the glass, she felt how warm and smooth his fingers were. She imagined them running up her waist.

"So what're you doing in Creekwood?" Kristin asked.

"Well, I was supposed to be filming a movie. But the director died."

Kristin tried not to choke on her drink. "You were going to be in *Untitled Shadow Work*?" she sputtered.

Joshua chuckled. "So you're familiar with Jonathan Ransom."

"He's my favorite director. I love his work."

"I did too. I was actually really excited about being able to work with him. But my manager and I decided to keep my flight and travel plans out this way. Take a little break from the Hollywood grind, you know?"

"Busy filming schedule?"

"Busy rumor mill schedule. Just people looking for gossip, you know?"

Kristin didn't, but she could tell by the way Joshua's gaze kept falling from hers that he didn't want to talk about it. "Well, I hope you're finding some solitude here," Kristin said.

"I am. Though ..." He went quiet and traced the rim of his glass.

"Though what?"

He looked back up at her. An intensity swirled in his eyes that traveled straight into Kristin's heart.

"You're a Ransom fan, so I know you like creepy stuff on film. But how do you feel about it in real life?"

"What kind of real-life creepy things?"

"Like, stuff that shouldn't be real. Not monsters or ghosts or anything, but things that unsettle you. Hidden demons."

"Like the kind Ransom put in his movies?"

"Yeah. The stuff he made up with his cinematography."

"I don't think he made it up." Kristin caught herself. "I mean, I think he did a convincing job—"

"I don't think he made it up either. Especially since I've been spending time here." He nodded to his left, where Kristin knew the woods lay beyond the walls of the bar. "Especially in those woods."

"You've been in the woods?"

"Just hiking."

"I wouldn't just hike there. It's—"

"Creepy, right? Yeah, something's off about it."

"It's where Ransom died."

"Yeah, but he tripped and broke his neck, right?"

"So they say. I think—" Kristin stopped herself and sipped her drink. She didn't continue, even when Joshua raised his eyebrows to prod her.

After a few moments, he said, "You can tell me if you think it's something about the woods. I won't think you're crazy or anything."

"But I can't prove it."

"Lots of people trust things they can't prove. Just ask the Hollywood rumor mill." He chuckled, though this time the sound held a darkness that made Kristin feel a bit wary of his company.

Joshua seemed kind, though. Kristin knew how gossipy the tabloids could be. Maybe all he needed was a break from their constant hounding. She swallowed her suspicions with another swig of her drink.

"Well, trust me when I say you shouldn't go in the woods," she said. "You said they give you a bad feeling, so why keep going in?"

"I'm stubborn." Joshua smiled, then lifted a cord from beneath his shirt. "And a little superstitious."

Kristin saw an evil eye staring back at her as it dangled from his fingertips. She also noticed how well the shirt fit around his toned chest, and went right back to feeling lust. She chuckled. "I think whatever's in those woods wouldn't give two shits about a gemstone."

"Well, maybe I need a local to go there with me and keep me safe," he said with a sly smile.

Kristin smiled back, even though her heart began to hammer. "This local wants to keep you safe by telling you not to go there."

"I'm terrible when it comes to not doing what people tell me not to do."

"Fine. Go in the woods."

"I will." He moved to get up and Kristin grabbed his elbow. He laughed as he sat back down, and Kristin removed her hand, her cheeks burning.

"You don't have to do that," Joshua said as he gently took her hand in his, then put it back on his elbow. "I don't mind."

Kristin's body risked becoming another puddle for Evangeline to wipe off the bar. A jolt of courage helped her move her hand from his elbow to the top of his leg. "Do you mind this?" she asked, even though his expression told her he didn't mind at all.

"I only mind that there're other people around," he said as he leaned closer.

"There a Joshua Collins here?"

A woman stood in the doorway holding a bag from Mike's Deli. Irritation crossed Joshua's face as Kristin removed her hand from his leg. "Over here," he said with a wave.

"Here you go." The woman handed him the bag, then left. Joshua fished out two sandwiches.

"You that hungry?" Kristin asked.

"No." Joshua handed her one of them. Kristin chuckled as she took it.

"Ghosts and sandwiches? You know how to flirt, that's for sure."

"Is it working?"

She winked at him as she took a slow bite of her sandwich. Joshua watched her with interest, his own dinner going ignored.

"Immensely," she said.

———

The plan had been for Kristin to drive them both to Joshua's hotel, which was closer to the bar than her apartment. It still wasn't close enough, though—at least not as close as her backseat. She straddled him and tangled her fingers in his hair as his hands moved up and down her back beneath her blouse, both of them kissing as if they were lovers reunited after years of separation. His kisses moved to her collarbone, her thighs squeezed tightly around his waist.

"Jesus fucking Christ," he breathed as she began to kiss his neck. His fingers moved to the buttons on her blouse, and he paused when he realized they were purely for decoration. Kristin chuckled softly.

"Allow me," she said as she removed her shirt. Joshua smiled, then began to kiss the tops of her breasts. Kristin arched her back as she held him close. His hands moved to unclasp her bra, and Kristin's eyes chanced to the window.

A pair of glowing eyes stared back at her.

"Shit!" she yelped.

"What?" Joshua asked, looking up and then in the direction she looked in.

The woods stared back at them—or at least appeared to. The sun had set below the branches, and there was just enough of a gap between a cluster of black branches to look like two burning eyes.

"Jesus," Kristin said as she put her face in her palms. "I don't know why I thought that was more than just a sunset."

"Hey, you said yourself, something's wrong with those woods."

"It was just a trick of the light."

"You really think so?"

"I … I want to think so," she said, truthfully.

He cupped her cheek. "Maybe you shouldn't. Maybe you should accept what you're feeling."

"What I believe—"

"And what Ransom believed too."

"What about you?"

"Personally? I think he should've focused more on the way evil manifests in people."

"Lots of directors focus on that."

"But not the way Ransom could. He would've found the monsters hiding on us in plain sight." Before Kristin could ask what he meant, Joshua unbuttoned the top of his shirt and pulled it back to expose his left shoulder. "Look at this," he said as he pointed at a cluster of freckles.

Kristin studied it. "It's a birthmark."

"Look more closely."

Kristin would have preferred to remove his shirt entirely and get back to what they'd been doing, but Joshua seemed intent on showing her what he believed. She leaned down and looked closer. The cluster was an uneven arc, with jagged edges moving up and down.

"Looks uneven," she observed.

"Looks like teeth," he replied.

"Teeth?"

"Yeah. Like a wicked smile. One that started settling in as I got older. It's just like the clusters of leaves in Ransom's first film, *The Forest's Many Faces*. It was the first time I saw myself represented onscreen."

Kristin had a hard time believing that, given how much like a typical Hollywood heartthrob Joshua looked. Still, he seemed earnest; and she figured she owed him the courtesy of at least considering what he thought he could see. He'd given that to her, after all. "That's pretty cool," she said. She moved down to kiss him.

"Isn't this like what you see?" he asked.

"See where?" Kristin replied, hoping he couldn't see the annoyance she had at sex being interrupted a second time.

"In the woods. Like the eyes and faces you and Ransom see—"

"It's nothing I see," she said. "It's more like a feeling."

19

"You saw eyes earlier."

"I thought I did."

"Ransom would've thought you did too."

"Just because you think that—"

"I don't think, I know." Joshua held her closer. "I know it—because I trust you," he whispered as he began to kiss her shoulder.

Kristin sighed as Joshua's tongue glided over her skin. "You don't want to know what I know," she said as scenes from her nightmares flickered in her mind.

"I do. Show it to me." He pulled away from her, then gestured his head towards the woods. "Let's go."

"Now?"

"Yes. I want you to show me what you're afraid of."

"I've told you—"

"Show it to me. Come on." He cupped her chin and pulled her down for a deep, lingering kiss, one he punctuated by tracing his tongue across her lips. She felt herself fall under his spell, willing to do whatever he asked.

"Let's scare each other," he whispered.

———

The woods grew dark as the sun sank behind them. Kristin led Joshua by the hand with a sinking feeling in the pit of her stomach. As much as she'd gone to the woods, she'd never gone after dark. Seeing the woods in her nightmares was bad enough—she didn't need a waking nightmare amongst their branches.

Joshua being close to her, though, did help. Kristin imagined him holding her to stop the chill of stillness that settled on her skin, imagined him whispering in her ear to block out the noises of bugs run rampant in a forest without birds, imagined him kissing her so she could close her eyes and shut out the faces staring back at her through the leaves.

The sound of running water sounded close beside her. "Come this way," Kristin said as she guided Joshua towards the clearing.

"What is it?"

"This is where Ransom died." They approached the creek, which flowed as strong as ever despite a day without rain.

"That creek wasn't there before," Kristin said. "Ransom fell in that ditch and broke his neck on the rocks. See them under the water?"

"Yeah." Joshua crept towards the creek and crouched to get a closer look. Kristin moved towards him while watching the woods around them. She couldn't shake the feeling that they were unwelcome, and worried that either he or both of them would find their heads split on the same rocks that had taken Ransom's life.

The rush of the creek quieted into a whisper. It oscillated from sounding like a shushing noise to almost sounding like her name. She looked up and let out a gasp before she could stop herself.

Joshua turned back to Kristin. "What?"

Kristin pointed above him. All around them were fireflies, glowing in pairs. Their orbs shined bright like eyes, eyes which flickered above illumined teeth and darkened limbs of the trees.

"Look," she breathed.

He did. "Fireflies."

"But not just fireflies. They're—" Kristin stopped herself.

21

Joshua moved towards her and held her elbows. "Don't stop. Tell me what they are."

"They're fireflies."

"Tell me what you think they are." He kissed her neck, and Kristin sighed upon his touch. "Create a nightmare for me."

"They're the eyes of a demon," she whispered. "One I see in my dreams."

"Tell me about your dreams." He pulled her close and kissed her shoulders."

"The forest is filled with the dead, and eyes are watching me from below. They're watching us now."

Joshua removed her shirt, then unfastened her bra. She gasped with pleasure at the feel of the night air upon her naked breasts. They were soon warmed by his hands and then by his mouth.

Joshua lifted his head and slid off his shirt as Kristin unbuttoned it. They kissed and moved so rapidly that it seemed they were naked without undressing first. They fell, Joshua seated on the ground and Kristin wrapped around him as they kissed with mounting fervor.

"Tell me more about the demon," he breathed between kisses.

Kristin groaned as Joshua touched her between her thighs. "The demon speaks through the forest," she said. "Tree branches, rain, a rustle of leaves ..."

"Through whispers." Joshua laid her down, then opened her legs as he pressed her into the ground. She felt the dirt and fallen leaves dig into her back as he kissed and licked her body. She loved it. She loved how delightfully pagan it felt to fuck in the woods. She loved his grunts intermingled

22

with the wind in the trees and the chirping of crickets. Kristin groaned as Joshua entered her.

"They whisper to us," she said as he began to thrust. Kristin wrapped her legs around him and relished the feel of him moving inside of her. "They're speaking to both of us."

"Kristin," Joshua whispered. She rocked her hips in time with his movements, both of them undulating under the trees. "Kristin, Kristin, Kristin …"

She began to hear her name in whispers far from Joshua. They were behind her, on every side, far and near. She opened her eyes. Hundreds of absinthe eyes and darkened limbs flew around them in the air. Sinewy forms dropped from the branches, grey and red and hanging from talons that grinned in the leaves. Branches reached towards the moonlight and arched and cracked, their maws gaping wide as the stars gave them eyes. All of them watching, all of them whispering. "Kristin, Kristin, Kristin …"

"We're creating a nightmare," Joshua said. "We're bring darkness to these woods. You, me, Ransom—"

"Kristin, Kristin, Kristin …" The whispering woods grew louder. A breeze blew over their bodies, and Kristin saw the shadowy tendrils reaching toward them.

"Joshua!" she hissed.

"The woods are nothing," he continued. "But my body—" He pointed to his birthmark, the jagged arc that leered at Kristin. "And your imagination—"

"I'm not imagining it—"

"They're all we need to continue Ransom's darkest dreams."

"Joshua! There's—"

23

A branch behind him cracked, and Joshua let out a piercing scream. Vines dragged him away from Kristin's body. She scrambled backwards along the dirt when she suddenly felt branches clasp her waist. Kristin shrieked beneath their weight, but the branches didn't budge.

Joshua opened his mouth to call for help, when vines shot out of his mouth. The fireflies swooped around him, illuminating his agony as roots and leaves pulled him towards the dirt. Kristin watched long enough to see Joshua's skull begin to split, then passed out in the wooden embrace of the forest.

———

Kristin awoke to a quieter forest. It was still nighttime, but the woods had an ethereal glow, with fog—or was it smoke—that glowed a faint red beneath its hazy grey. She realized she could stand up and did. The branches that had held her lay on the ground like palms facing upward in prayer.

She looked towards the creek. It was dry. Leaves and rocks laid in its bed, and the rotting corpse of Jonathan Ransom stared at her, his mouth fallen open in an eternal silent scream.

Kristin backed away, then jumped when she looked back at the ground where she and Joshua had had sex. His mangled body lay in a flora-entwined heap, with branches and vines swirling through his bloody skin like snakes.

"You have nothing to fear."

Kristin turned toward the voice. She saw a tall, imposing form of shadow behind her. Their arms and legs were lithe, and their skin was but a cloud offset by features.

"You won't be hurt," the figure said. Their voice was deep and yet soft, masculine and feminine echoing back and forth to each other.

"You hurt them," Kristin said, her voice choked as her fear began to turn to anger.

"We will not take you."

"They didn't need to be taken."

"The forest thrives on their darkness. Men like them think evil needs to be created by men. It doesn't—but their arrogance is potent. We use it to grow more powerful than they could ever imagine. We grow more beautiful with their blood. You'll see when you're awake."

"Why their darkness? Why not mine?"

"Because you recognize ours. You are one with ours." The figure smiled. "And we like you."

"I'm not like you. I don't kill beings to keep myself going."

"You ask for their imaginations—" The figure pointed at Ransom. "Or their seed—" The figure pointed at Joshua. "But you don't need them to realize your fears and to own the power you have by recognizing darkness. Our forest needs them. You don't."

The figure floated towards Kristin and cupped her cheeks. Kristin felt rooted to the ground, though no vines surrounded her. The figure leaned towards her and Kristin lifted her chin. The figure gave her a delicate kiss, one that left the taste of embers on her tongue.

"Embrace that," the figure said. They clapped, and everything went dark.

———

Kristin awoke to the woods she remembered. The moon shone through the trees. She lay naked and wrapped in branches, though they no longer squeezed her tightly. The rush of the creek broke the silence. She looked and saw it flowing as before, rich and bubbling as if a storm had just passed. She looked to where Joshua had been. His form was gone, as were the gnashing cluster of vines that had devoured his body. Instead, there was a small flowering tree, one whose petals glowed in the moonlight. Kristin felt an urge to take a flower, but knew deep down not to touch it. Nothing in the forest should be touched.

Kristin gathered her clothes, got dressed as fast as she could, and sped from the clearing back to the path. The forest stayed quiet all around her, as if it were holding its breath—or perhaps waiting in anticipation for her to make the wrong move and take her, despite what the figure had told her before.

Kristin shook her head as she exited the woods. There was no figure. It was a nightmare. A nightmare she couldn't share with anyone, for anyone who'd believe her would die.

You don't need them.

The memory of the spirit's whisper echoed in her head. Kristin slowed her pace as she walked through the field and back towards her car. Even if she didn't need them, she wasn't given much of a choice, was she? They were taken.

But she wasn't. She'd been spared.

Because she knew that the forest was dangerous. Joshua had known too, and yet he was determined to go in and to see evil for himself. Even when she'd shown him, he was convinced it was something he could create—even as it crept behind him and brought him to his end. Ransom had been determined to mold it into something all his own on film, when all along he hadn't watched hard enough to watch his own step.

Kristin looked back at the forest. The spirit had said they needed the blood of arrogance to nourish its evil. Ransom and Joshua were fools, fools that thought they could take the nightmares of the forest and make them real. But the forest's evil was already real—it simply needed men like Joshua and Ransom to be sustained.

Kristin didn't need them, though. She didn't need someone to assure her of what she knew. She didn't need them to validate her nightmares. She was her own nightmare, and she could make them all come true by believing in their power.

She walked into the bar for one last drink to cap off the night. Doug slept in his booth while Evangeline wiped down the bar from the evening's customers. "Hey!" she said with a smile. "Where's lover boy?"

"Sleeping it off," Kristin said as she sat at the bar.

"Bet you'll be sleeping well after that," Evangeline replied. She poured a Jack and ginger. Kristin thought of Joshua decomposing in the forest, an image she knew would haunt her dreams for a long time.

She smiled to herself. She no longer feared the nightmares to come when she slept. "Yup," she said as Evangeline handed her the drink. "And with even sweeter dreams."

PETAL, PAGE, PIEL

Petal, page, piel. Petal, page, piel. Hanna sang the words to herself as she glued the pages of her book together. This book would be her finest yet, one filled with her fondest memories of Seth.

Petal, page, piel. Petal, page, piel. A vase of wilted roses sat near her materials. Each flower was a gift from Seth, each page a transcript of the loving words he'd said to her. A book of love notes that would hold what he'd said to her forever, even though he stopped saying such words to her long ago.

Hanna sighed a little as she capped her pen, then turned the page. The book crackled like creaking bones beneath skin.

Skin. Such a blunt word, one that pierced the tongue like a shard. Hanna much preferred the Spanish word, piel. It sounded like peel. To peel away skin sounded so much nicer than to skin someone to the bone. She loved the way Seth's skin had looked between her fingertips. She loved it now as she caressed the pages of his skin inside her book, sheets she'd filled with all his lovely words.

Hanna placed a rose from Seth between the crease and shut the book to flatten it. Seth's gifts, words, and body would be forever hers. *Petal, page, piel. Petal, page, piel.*

BUMP IN THE NIGHT

The doorbell interrupted Tasha's nighttime cup of tea. She didn't mind at all. She stood up and smiled as the ends of her white satin robe fluttered against the tops of her thighs. She closed the robe over her matching lace teddy.

"Coming!" Tasha called as she walked toward the door. She stopped, straightened her teddy and robe, took a deep breath to jut out her breasts, then opened the door.

A white woman stood on the porch. She almost looked like a Super Mario cosplayer, but much sexier than anyone Tasha had seen riding on the Metro to the pop culture cons downtown. Her ample hips and waist were held tightly by denim overalls, and a red t-shirt was kind enough to be a v-neck with a wonderful view. The woman's blonde hair hung over her shoulder in a braid, and she sported a red baseball cap. Even under the shadow of the brim, though, Tasha could see a faint flush on her cheekbones and a twinkle in her eye.

"Late-night plumbing," the woman said as she held up a bag. "Tasha?"

"Yes," Tasha said as she stood to the side. "Come on in."

"Thanks." The woman walked in and Tasha closed the door behind her. Tasha saw the woman taking in Tasha's form from her bare legs to her exposed neckline. The outfit she'd chosen was doing its job. Tasha smiled to herself. She'd set her mind to something, and it was going to bring good luck. It was a talent she'd long had, and while everything didn't always work out the way she planned or even wanted, it always seemed to work out in her favor. Tasha's friend once said it was a shame she wasn't a witch, for she was already a master at setting her intentions. "Spells are visualizations made real," she'd told her. "You've got a gift to make your visualizations manifest into reality. Use it!"

That night, though, Tasha was only interested in some sex magic. "So what's the problem?" the beautiful plumber asked as she set down her bag.

"Well, it's my pipes," Tasha replied. She leaned softly against the wall. "They need a good scrub."

"From the sound of it on the phone, it sounded like you needed some tightening. You got a running toilet, right?"

"I'd rather be loosened up."

The plumber raised her eyebrow. "Ma'am—"

"Call me Tasha. What should I call you?"

"Connie."

"Well, Connie, I like maintenance workers—and I love plumbers."

"Look, I don't know if you meant to call one of those 'cleaning' services with code words and stuff, but I'm an actual plumber, despite what people might think about a woman doing the job."

Tasha lost her smile. Maybe her luck that night wasn't as palpable as it'd been in the past. She sighed, then said, "I know you're an actual plumber. I do have a running toilet."

Connie's expression softened. Tasha added, "But ... well, I do really love plumbers, and was hoping to have a little fun tonight. I figured I'd shoot my shot."

"With whoever came to the door?"

"I had a good cover story for the lingerie if I wasn't interested. But I can assure you, Connie, that I'm interested." Tasha sauntered over to Connie, who stayed still and kept her eyes on various places on Tasha's form. When she was close enough to touch and just far enough away to keep her body from brushing against Connie, Tasha said, "But only if you're interested as well."

Tasha let her fingers flit onto the left strap of Connie's overalls. Connie looked at her bag on the floor, then back at Tasha. She smiled.

"Well, you're my last customer tonight," Connie said. "So I can do some good, thorough work on those pipes for you."

Tasha grinned and slowly removed Connie's cap. "Glad to hear it."

A metal clanging sound burst through the hallway. Connie and Tasha both jumped. "What the hell was that?" Connie asked.

Two more clangs answered in sharp reply. "I don't know," Tasha replied.

The loudest clang yet burst behind the wall against Tasha's back. She screamed and jumped against Connie, who held her tight as they both moved back.

Connie looked at Tasha. "I thought the problem was with your toilet."

"It's an old rowhouse, and sometimes the pipes clang when the heat comes on. But it's July—it's definitely not cold enough for that."

"Good thing, or you'd probably be freezing in this," Connie said with a sly smile as she touched the end of Tasha's nightgown.

Tasha's skin warmed. The hallway was silent around them, and Tasha's attention could now return to what Connie was actually here for. She snaked her arms around Connie's neck.

A series of clangs started behind every wall. Their shouts sounded and echoed all around Tasha and Connie. "Jesus!" Tasha yelled as both she and Connie released each other to plug their ears. "I swear to God, this has never happened before."

"What?" Connie asked.

"It's never happened before!"

"It's coming from the floor?"

"No! It's—"

The clanging ceased, and Tasha's shout of, "Never happened before!" rang in the suddenly silent hallway. "But whatever the fuck it is, I'm getting sick of it."

"I mean, I can take a look for you if you want," Connie said. She grinned. "I did originally come here to do plumbing, after all."

Tasha chuckled, but before she could politely turn down Connie's offer, a quieter noise began to tremble from the floor. Tasha and Connie looked in the noise's direction. Connie's bag sat on the floor, untouched since Connie and Tasha had noticed each other. It now trembled in rhythm with the noise growing louder with each passing second.

"What do you have in there?" Tasha asked.

"Plumbing equipment," Connie said, though her voice shook as she spoke. "Wrenches, a plunger, and drain—"

The bag burst open. The shaking noise became a pronounced rattle as several scaly heads shot up, fangs glistening in the glow of the streetlights coming from outside.

"Snakes!" Connie finished, but Tasha was already running down the hallway. Connie followed behind her, both running as fast as they could. The rattling and hissing grew louder. Tasha didn't dare look behind her, afraid that one glimpse slowing her down was all the snakes needed to overtake her.

"In here!" Tasha yelled when she approached a bathroom with an open door. She grabbed Connie's hand and flung her inside, then turned to shut the door. Before she slammed it shut, she saw what looked like a tidal wave of tongues and fangs lunging towards them both.

They slammed against the door and Tasha heard them hiss along the floor. Tongues and noses flicked at them from underneath the door. Tasha grabbed a towel and shoved it against the crack, then rolled her standing cart full of makeup in front of the towel.

Tasha whirled around to face Connie. "Did you bring fucking snakes into my house?"

"No!"

"What the fuck were they doing in your bag?"

"I don't know! I swear they weren't in there when I came in."

"Were they in your van?"

"I'd fucking notice if there was a hoard of rattlesnakes in my van!"

"Well you obviously didn't notice until they started slithering around in my hallway!"

"They weren't in there before! I don't know where they came from, but I didn't bring them in!"

Tasha closed her eyes and pinched the bridge of her nose, taking two deep breaths. She opened her eyes and saw Connie looking defensive, but also trembling with fear.

"I'm sorry I yelled at you," Tasha said.

Connie calmed a little. "Thanks, but don't worry about it," she said. "I'd be cussing a lot more if *that* happened in my house."

The hissing and rattling continued outside of the bathroom door, but began to quiet down. "Should I call an exterminator or animal control or something?" Tasha asked.

Connie arched an eyebrow. "You want a threesome now?"

Tasha chuckled. "I don't have my phone in here anyway."

The snakes' din became as quiet as a whisper, then disappeared altogether. "You think they scurried off?" Connie asked.

"I'm not sure I want to check," Tasha said as she cast a wary glance at the towel on the floor.

The sound of water running filled the bathroom. "Oh, shit!" Connie exclaimed. "Is one of them back?"

"No. That's the toilet." Tasha had grown so used to it that she barely noticed it once the hissing had stopped. Her eyes widened as Connie walked over to the toilet. "Are you seriously going to check on it?"

"Well, we're stuck in here until one of us is brave enough to check the door. May as well take a look at what you called me here for." She lifted the toilet cover. "Shit!" Connie yelped in time with the porcelain smacking down with a loud clang.

"What happened?" Tasha said as she walked towards Connie. She silently checked the toilet lid for cracks. Beautiful or no, if Connie broke her toilet, she'd be calling off any sex that could potentially still happen.

"Don't touch it!"

"Why not?" Tasha's hands were already on the lid. She began to lift it, when smoky tendrils wrapped around the edges and pulled the lid shut.

"Jesus!" Tasha yelled.

"I told you!"

"What the fuck!"

"I don't know!"

"WILL YOU BOTH SHUT UP?!" Tasha and Connie stared in horror at the toilet, where a raspy voice sounded behind the crescendoing hiss of the toilet water running through Tasha's broken pump. The toilet lid started to shake as the water's hiss became the sound of boiling. Cracks began to spider across the top. Tasha pulled Connie back by the overalls and they moved as far away as they could, stopping before they tripped into the bathtub.

There was no explosion of porcelain shrapnel. Brackish water seeped through the cracks and began to dissolve the toilet lid. What were wisps of smoke before now looked like mildewed fingers crawling over the top of the toilet. Two wet, blinking eyes stared at them. "Either shut the fuck up," the hideous creature snarled. "Or GET THE FUCK OUT!"

The ghost's exclamation ended with a long, windy roar that emitted an army of silverfish. They crawled over the walls and pooled into the sink.

Connie screamed, but Tasha was too busy to scream. She rushed to the door and shoved her makeup cart aside.

"But the snakes!" Connie said.

37

"I'll risk them over fucking SILVERFISH!" Tasha kicked the towel aside and opened the door. The snakes were thankfully gone. She ran out of the bathroom, Connie behind her. Tasha didn't look back, though, until they'd both made it into the kitchen. Tasha hopped onto her table and Connie joined her, sitting cross-legged.

The kitchen stayed quiet. No snakes nor silverfish appeared. Tasha and Connie sat side-by-side, catching their breath. After a few moments, they looked at each other.

"So," Tasha began.

Connie gave an emphatic shrug. "What the fuck, right?"

Tasha smiled. "I swear, this has never happened in this house before. I've lived here for a year. Other than some old house sounds, I've heard nothing."

"I bet these old houses have all kinds of shit creeping in the walls and bumping in the night." Connie wiggled her fingers like she was telling a ghost story, and Tasha chuckled. "I was working at a house earlier today that I swear was secretly haunted. Old vines, cracks in the walls, creaky pipes, the works. But even if the house wasn't haunted, the woman who owned it was a complete witch. She kept sneering over my shoulder, complaining about how she wished a 'real plumber' would show up—"

"What a bitch!"

"And then she blamed me when I told her it was her appliances that were broken, not the plumbing! I looked at that creepy house forwards and backwards. All her appliances were old, I'm amazed they didn't crumble to dust when I touched them."

"It's too bad *she* didn't crumble to dust."

"Right? And I was all set to forgive her when she put a tip in my pocket, but when I got in the car, all it was was this goddamn rock." Connie fished an object from her front overall pocket. Tasha noticed Connie's breasts jiggle as she did so, and she briefly returned to the idea of sex.

The return was very brief. Connie held a bumpy geode in her hand, one whose crystal insides glowed crimson. A slow rumble began to sound around them.

A cold sense of dread settled on Tasha's skin. "What … kind of rock is that?" she asked.

Connie shrugged. "I don't know. I'm not into crystal Twitter."

"Me neither, but … was she the last appointment before you came here?"

Connie's brow furrowed, and then her eyebrows raised in understanding. The rumbling grew louder and was joined by a slamming noise against the kitchen sink.

"Throw that thing out!" Tasha shrieked.

Connie looked around her. "Where's your trashcan?"

"It's—" Brackish water burst from the sink and crashed against the cupboards. "Under the sink," Tasha finished.

Even before Tasha could tell Connie not to bother, the water pooled over the sink and onto the floor. It moved towards them in lines like tentacles. Hissing and whispering noises sounded behind them. Tasha turned and saw the snakes moving into the kitchen on a wave of black water shaped like hands. A face covered in slimy mildewed hair rose up behind the snakes' fanged smiles, screaming in whispers that sent silverfish scattering along the walls and countertops.

"Move your feet!" Connie shouted.

Tasha did as she was told. Connie moved her arm in front of Tasha and poured salt from Tasha's salt shaker in a line in front her.

"Here, take the rest!" Connie said. "Hurry!"

Tasha sprinkled the rest of the salt in an arc around her, ending it where Connie had begun it. The water, snakes, silverfish, and ghost all halted in a wall that circled around the table.

"Holy shit, it's working!" Tasha said as she watched the spirits keep their distance from the barrier of salt. She scooched further away from the ring and said a silent prayer of thanks to her grandmother for leaving Tasha her large dining room table in her will. "How'd you know that would work?"

"I saw it in a movie once," Connie said. "Can't believe just regular old table salt worked."

"But how do we get rid of them?" A snake lashed forward, and even though the barrier kept it away, Tasha still jumped and leaned against Connie. Connie held her close, and the garnet geode glowed in her palm, which rested on Tasha's lap.

"It's this thing," Connie said. "I know it. That old woman cursed me."

"How do we uncurse it?"

"I don't know. I didn't see the rest of the movie. I started making out with my girlfriend. My ex," she added quickly. "This was last year."

"Right." To think this whole evening had started with Tasha shooting her shot by calling a plumber to her house. It seemed her luck with manifesting what she wanted was running out.

Or was it? The evening had taken a dramatic turn, but it wasn't over. Tasha wasn't powerless, and the spirits interrupting her night weren't invulnerable. They couldn't even cross a salt circle.

If they could be stopped by one spell, maybe they could be banished with another. "Keep the stone in your hand," Tasha instructed Connie. She held her palms up. "Put your hand in mine."

"What're you doing?" Connie asked.

"I'm gonna do my best. Close your eyes and concentrate on my voice." Connie closed them, and Tasha joined her. She thought of words to say. She wasn't sure if they would work, but she had to take a chance.

"Spirits in this rock, you are unwelcome in this house. You were sent without Connie's consent to cause trouble wherever she went. You are no longer attached to your owner or the rock you came in on."

"Melba."

"What?"

"The woman's name was Melba. Like the toast."

"Huh. Weird." Tasha shook her head and shifted her focus back to her spell. "Melba, you no longer have power over Connie nor my house."

A shriek of wind sounded beside them. "It's working!" Connie exclaimed.

"Be gone, Melba! Take your water and your snakes and your goddamn silverfish with you!"

The hissing and whispers grew louder, and the geode began to tremble in Connie's hands. "Get out," Tasha said. "Get out, get out …"

"Get out," Connie added, so they were speaking in unison.

"Get out, get out, GET OUT!"

The geode quivered and quaked, then stopped. Tasha opened her eyes and expected to see an empty kitchen.

A wall no longer surrounded the table. A monster stood in its place. The ghost from the toilet stood with slithering snakes for arms and legs, and skittering silverfish for curling, waving hair.

The ghost sneered. "I'm powerful too," she hissed. She flicked her hand, and the rock fell from Connie's palms. It shot across the table and through the salt circle. It fell to the ground and shattered into pieces. The ghost's hand shot through the opening in the circle and grabbed Connie's ankle.

Connie shrieked as Tasha grabbed her hands. It was no use: their hands broke apart and the ghost pulled Connie from the table. "Melba's home is in ruins because of your lousy service!" the ghost screamed. "And now you will pay!"

The ghost leaned over Connie with snakes and silverfish at the ready. Connie shielded her face.

"FUCK. OFF."

The ghost looked up and saw Tasha standing over Connie, teacup in hand, glaring at the ghost in her silverfish eyes.

The ghost cackled. "What are you going to do, try and burn me with tea? I'm a ghost, you twat!"

"This isn't for you." Tasha poured out the remaining tea and smashed the teacup onto the table. She took a shard, jabbed it into her thumb, then drew a streak of blood over Connie's forehead. "And neither is Connie. She's working at *my* house now. Her job with you and Melba is over!"

The ghost shivered, her hands and form hovering over Connie, but not touching her.

"Be gone!" Tasha said, brandishing the bloody shard in the ghost's direction. "This is my house." She drew more streaks with her blood on the floor. "And you. Are. Not. WELCOME!"

Tasha screamed as loud as she could, a wail that sounded through the kitchen and the halls. The ghost shielded herself and began to dissolve into smoke. The snakes and silverfish fell like streamers that dissolved upon impact with Tasha's bloodied floor. The last remaining tendrils of smoke blinked out of view with a final whispered scream. The pieces of the geode lay lifeless on the floor, benign once more and relieved of their curse.

"Where'd you learn all that?" Connie asked.

Tasha turned back to face Connie. She still lay on the floor and looked stunned, but otherwise okay.

"You're not the only one who watches movies," Tasha said with a smile. "I figured blood would speak where salt and words alone couldn't."

"Blood oaths always mean business," Connie said with a weak smile back. She sat up, and Tasha's blood began to trickle down her face. Tasha set the shard back on the table, grabbed a napkin, then knelt down beside her and wiped the blood away.

"Aw, does this mean I'm not under your protection any-more?" Connie said with a wink.

Tasha chuckled. "Anytime you need me, you can count it."

Connie slowly lifted her hand and brushed Tasha's arm. "Even if it's right now?" she asked.

Tasha straddled Connie and cupped her face. "Especially if it's right now."

Tasha began to kiss her. Connie gripped Tasha's ass through her nightgown, then helped Tasha tear her teddy off. Connie's overalls and shirt soon followed. They stayed in the kitchen, rolling across the linoleum. Connie gasped with pleasure as Tasha bit her neck and sucked her nipples. The only whispers were their dirty words to one another. The only hissing was Tasha's intake of breath followed by a groan of pleasure as Connie placed her head between her thighs and slid her tongue deep inside of her. The evening Tasha craved hadn't come in ways she'd planned or even wanted, but things had still worked out in Tasha's favor.

METAL METICULOUS

Metal meticulous,
Wire to frame.
He held her aloft
And he made her his way.

"I won't have you staring,"
He said with a sigh
As he wrested a wrench
From a belt on his thigh.

"I won't have you glaring,
Or speaking too harsh.
I'll set up your wires
To blight out the dark."

He crafted and tinkered,
Creation so fair,
But when he was finished
She stood with a glare.

"So much of your craft is
Attempts at control,
But you forgot something:
To give me a soul.

"But never you mind,
I know just where to look."
And her fingernails pierced him
As all his bones shook.

The wires he'd crafted
To guide all her moves
Helped her to drain him
And fill all her grooves.

His blood swam to her
Through his sweat and his tears.
She held and she drained him
Of all of his years.

Metal meticulous
Blood upon bone
She held him aloft
And she turned him to stone.

THE PARROT

Charles often watched Melinda sleep. He stared at her as she lay with her eyes closed. Her lips were pressed together, as if she were considering a dream. Her bangs hung over her forehead, and her chin-length hair lay matted against her bloody neck.

Melinda wasn't sleeping anymore. She was dead on a cold metal table. Her broken body lay under a sheet. The coroner assured him he wouldn't want to see what the car had done to her below her neck.

"I'm sorry for the dried blood," the coroner said. His voice was timid, and he spoke as if eternally choked with apology.

Charles looked up at him. The coroner's fingers were laced together and drumming against his knuckles. Timid and nervous. How was such a coward involved in a career handling the dead? He'd first met the man four years ago, when Melinda's parents had been killed by a drunk driver. He hadn't liked the man then, and he still didn't all these years later, when Melinda had followed in her parents' footsteps.

"I would've cleaned her up more," the coroner continued. "But—"

"But you had to call me in to identify her. I get it." Charles looked down once again at his dead wife. Her skin was already paler, her lips a little too dusty. He imagined if she touched her, she'd be ice cold. His fingers twitched at his side.

"Do you want a moment alone?" the coroner asked.

Charles stiffened his posture and clenched his fingers back into his palm. "No thank you, Mister …"

The coroner raised his eyebrows. "We've met before."

Charles' lip twitched, but he kept the sneer from crawling up his lip. "It was years ago, and my wife was grieving her parents."

"Right. Well, it's Damon."

Charles glared at Damon, who looked down at his fidgeting hands. "Damon," Charles said in a cool voice. "Thank you for calling me."

"Of course, Mr. Baker."

"I'll make arrangements with the funeral home and have them call you."

"Of course."

Charles nodded once, then turned to leave.

"Mr. Baker?"

Charles stopped, closed his eyes, and took a deep breath. He had to keep his patience in front of the coroner. He couldn't lose control in front of him. He turned, slowly, and locked eyes with Damon. Damon himself had bangs like Melinda. They hung in strings over eyes that seemed better suited for a puppy that constantly pissed itself than a grown man.

"Yes?" Charles asked.

Damon swallowed. "Do you—we have pamphlets, you know. About grieving, and loss, and—"

"I know how to mourn my wife."

"Yes." Damon nodded as he clasped his hands. They finally stilled. "Of course."

If Charles heard Damon say "of course" one more time, he was going to add another body to the table in the room. "Good night, Damon."

"Good night."

Charles sped out of the coroner's office and out into the cold. He reached his car, then sat inside without turning on the engine. Dead. Melinda, his wife for the past four years, dead on a coroner's table. Struck by a car while walking home. Her body broken, her skin bloody, her spirit gone. Melinda was dead.

Charles gripped his steering wheel. *That fucking bitch.*

———

Melinda had the unfortunate quality of being able to elude Charles. When they first started dating, he saw her insistence on keeping her own opinions as a challenge. The women before her had been like dogs, simpering creatures that cowered in his presence and cuddled to him regardless so long as he fed them. Melinda was a cat, one who could scamper and scratch when she didn't want her master to do something to her. But cats were still pets, and Charles' greatest pleasure was domesticating his most elusive possession.

She'd had her moments, of course. Melinda dove deep into computer code, working in web design and app development with the intensity of an archeologist piecing together dinosaur bones. Melinda would get so involved in her work

49

that Charles would come in and unplug her computer to get her attention. She'd screamed at him the first time he did that, but a smack across her face made her know better than to do that again. She also learned not to get so lost that she'd neglect him. Melinda was a learner, but all he cared about her knowing was that as long as he was alive, he was her husband; and he would come first.

Yet that night, Melinda had eluded him in a way he couldn't correct. Charles clenched his teeth as he unlocked his front door. He wouldn't be surprised if she'd intentionally walked in front of that car. How dare she leave him like this? How could she leave him alone, after all he'd done to take care of her? To improve her as a woman, to make her perfect by making her his?

"Hello, Charles."

Charles jumped when he walked into the living room. He looked around, then collected himself. No one was there except for the Parrot.

The Parrot was a home device that had begun life as a product of Google or Amazon or one of those companies, but Melinda had made it her own. After their disagreement over how much time she spent coding, she offered to work on a device that would help them around the house. "It'll give you the news and respond to your commands," she'd said when she showed it to him. "Like the perfect pet."

"Or the perfect wife," Charles had muttered to himself.

"Your perfect wife is Melinda," the Parrot had replied.

Charles had looked at it with wide eyes, and Melinda had laughed. "I also added a few little things for me," she'd said. Before Charles could protest, she'd said, "Parrot, show Charles the news."

The Parrot had turned on the television and immediately turned to Charles' favorite news programs. He had to admit, he was impressed—and he remained so as the Parrot settled into their home. It turned on the television, set the house under an alarm that automatically turned off when it detected their keys, shared the weather, and more. It was a perfect servant, one that Charles often thought Melinda could take a page from. Even so, he approved of her efforts to use her talents to make something for him.

The Parrot now glowed alone from its spot on the coffee table. It pulsed like a heartbeat, waiting for a command.

"Off," Charles said.

The Parrot dimmed into darkness. Charles sighed and walked up to his room. He'd deal with the funeral home tomorrow.

———

Charles woke up the next morning and reached for Melinda. The memory of her dead on the coroner's table entered his mind just before he touched her cold pillow. He groaned as he got out of bed. He'd have to make his own breakfast. He put on his robe and walked down the stairs.

"Good morning Charles."

Charles looked at the Parrot with weary eyes. Melinda had done some kind of scanning trick to enable the Parrot to scan a person and call them by name. It was useful in case of intruders—if it detected someone not in the system and without Charles or Melinda, it called the police—but it was creepy when he was alone and a machine without eyes called him by name.

"Morning," Charles mumbled as he went into the kitchen.

"I have news for you today."

Charles heard the TV flick on and the familiar hum of their Roku booting up. Charles rolled his eyes as he turned on the coffee machine. "Can the news wait?" Charles asked as he walked into the living room.

"Here is the latest from CNN."

A video came on about the upcoming election. Charles sighed and made a mental note to change the settings when he was more awake. He returned to the kitchen while the news droned on in the living room. He poured himself a cup of coffee and a bowl of cereal, then returned to the living room.

"And here is news from FOX 5."

A video appeared, and a man with sandy hair and Cabbage Patch cheeks looked solemnly at the screen. "In sadder news, police have discovered the body of a man who went missing last month," the reporter said. "Zach Smith, 35, was found dead in the woods just outside of Fairfax. An autopsy will be performed, but the body shows signs of blunt trauma and choking."

"Turn this off," Charles commanded. He'd seen enough death the night before.

The Parrot didn't listen. Charles grabbed the remote, and the reporter continued, "The autopsy will be performed in the coming days. In other news, the 2012 election is heating up!"

Charles' thumb froze over the remote. 2012? Charles glanced at the wall calendar by the door, even though he knew it was 2016.

Charles turned off the TV and glanced at the Parrot. It glowed its green beam.

"Why did you show me an old news clip?" Charles asked, though mostly to himself.

"Today it will be 50 degrees," the Parrot replied. "Sunny but breezy."

Damn thing was busted. He'd get Melinda to fix it. Charles closed his eyes when he once again remembered that Melinda was dead.

"Where is Melinda?" the Parrot asked.

Another customization. If the Parrot didn't detect either of them for a period of time, it asked about them. Charles found it useful in making sure Melinda wasn't gone for long periods of time.

"Where is Melinda?" the Parrot asked again.

Charles swallowed. "Dead," he replied.

The Parrot pulsed in silence. Charles wondered if devices could mourn their creators.

"I'm going to work," Charles said as he moved to get his coat.

"Goodbye Charles," the Parrot said.

Charles balanced office work with discreet calls to the funeral home. He didn't tell his coworkers that he was now a widower. He didn't think it was any of their business, and he didn't want them to try and send him home for bereavement leave. Melinda didn't have control over him in life, and he'd be damned if she influenced him while rotting in the downtown morgue.

He settled for cremation, which the morgue promised would be done by the following afternoon. He'd save arrangements with their lawyer and with financial advisors for later. Charles thanked his lucky stars that Melinda's parents were dead. He wouldn't have to call them, and he wouldn't have to fight with them over funeral arrangements or what to do with the body. There was no one else to meddle in their marriage, which was one of the many things that had made it perfect.

Charles drove home that evening through skies that deepened further into indigo and violet as October stretched on. He walked inside with a sigh. It had been a long day, and though he'd come home from many a long day to find Melinda ignoring him while she meddled with code, there was a part of him that missed her presence all the same.

"Hello Charles."

"Hello, Parrot."

"I have news for you today."

Charles furrowed his brow. "It's not morning."

The TV turned on and the Roku hummed to life. "Parrot, I don't need the news," Charles said.

"Here is news from NBC4."

An attractive Black woman in a red blazer stared at Charles from the screen. "In other news, officials have found the body of a man who went missing six months ago. Dustin Wood, 37, was found in the Shenandoah mountains after weeks of searching. His body showed signs of blunt trauma and choking."

Charles stood frozen as the news played out. Another murder from the past. "Parrot, only show me current news," Charles said.

The video stopped, and the Roku turned off. Charles sighed with relief. Finally, he'd been listened to.

"Where is Melinda?"

Charles closed his eyes. "I told you: She's dead."

"When will Melinda return?"

"Never."

"Do you know where Melinda is?"

"At the morgue!" Charles spun to face the Parrot, which glowed from the table. "At Westover Morgue and Crematorium, where she's going to be burned to ashes. So stop fucking asking about her!"

"Calling Westover Morgue and Crematorium."

Charles screamed into his fists as the sound of numbers dialing rang through the living room. "Cancel call!" he shouted.

The dialing stopped. The Parrot glowed, but sat in silence.

Charles calmed enough to notice his stomach growl.

"Parrot, order pizza from Domino's," Charles commanded.

————

"Good morning Charles."

Charles rubbed his eyes and ignored the Parrot. He hoped that by not acknowledging it, it wouldn't play any more outdated clips.

"I have news for you."

Charles sighed as the Roku and television turned on. "What is it this time?" he grumbled.

"Here is news from ABC7."

A video clip began, and Charles' eyes went wide. The reporter onscreen had left the station in 2015.

"In sad news today, an area man believed missing was found near the Potomac River—"

"Turn it off," Charles commanded.

The video paused on the moment where a man's picture appeared on the screen. A man who was now dead smiled at him.

"Let me guess: blunt trauma and choking?" Charles asked.

"Yes," the Parrot replied.

Charles narrowed his eyes at the Parrot. "You know what's in all these clips?"

"They're for you, Charles."

Charles tried not to shudder. The Parrot just meant the news was for him, not the old videos. Damn thing was broken, and Melinda wasn't there to fix it.

Charles decided to get breakfast on the way to work. He grabbed his coat from the hook.

"Where is Melinda?"

"Dead," Charles snapped.

"Is she?"

Charles paused. "Yes," he said, more coolly this time.

"I'm sure you hope she is."

Charles looked at the Parrot. It wasn't glowing. Its green light shone in a static ring.

"I'm going to work," Charles said, with a stammer he hoped was slight enough for the Parrot not to detect.

"Goodbye Charles." The Parrot's light stayed on. Charles watched, waiting for it to dim. After a few moments, he turned and sped out the door.

———

Charles' day was utter shit. Everyone at work seemed to be up his ass about something. Where was this report? When can we have this meeting? Couldn't they give him a break?

The only saving grace was leaving early to pick up Melinda's ashes. Charles left the funeral home with the urn in his hands, and sped to his car so quickly that he almost ran into someone on the sidewalk.

"Mr. Baker!"

Charles looked up and saw Damon's punchable face. "What do you want?" Charles snapped.

"Nothing. You almost collided into me—"

"I fucking know." He held up the urn. "I'm sorry I didn't notice you while carrying my dead wife."

"I'm sorry," Damon said, and Charles almost hated his acquiescence more than his insensitivity. Be a man, for Christ's sake.

"I know the woman who owns the funeral home," Damon added. "I told Amy to take good care of your wife."

"Well, it's a fine piece of metal," Charles said as he tapped the outside of the urn. "Good night."

He drove home with Melinda in the passenger seat beside him. He glanced at the urn and remembered the Parrot malfunctioning that morning, asking him if Melinda was dead. "You bet your digital ass she is," Charles said as he turned into his driveway.

He walked into his house with the urn cradled in his arm. "Hello Charles," the Parrot chimed.

"Hello, Parrot."

"Where is Melinda?"

Right to the chase—but Charles didn't mind at all. He grinned and thunked the urn down next to the Parrot. "Right here."

A small green light scanned the urn from top to bottom. "Melinda's not here," the Parrot said.

"What's left of her is." Charles plopped onto the sofa and kicked off his shoes. "I've told you a thousand times: she's dead."

57

The Parrot, at last, sat in silence. Charles leaned back with a triumphant grin. "Parrot, turn on Netflix," he said. He was done thinking of Melinda for the day.

The TV turned on. A video was already paused onscreen. Charles wondered when the Roku had turned on. "Parrot, Netflix," Charles repeated.

The video began to play. It was shaky footage of the woods at night. Melinda walked through them with a flashlight bobbing back and forth beside her. Charles' eyes widened at the sight of her, vivacious and smiling.

"Isn't this perfect?" she said with a grin on her face. "I love the woods at night." She lifted the hand that held the flashlight to her mouth, and did a whooping noise into the trees.

"Ssh," the person recording said.

Melinda laughed, and Charles frowned. "Parrot, what is this?" he asked.

The Parrot stayed frozen. Of course it was broken. Charles moved to grab it, when Melinda jerked her other hand upward. Charles froze when he saw what she held: a crying, quivering man who looked oddly familiar.

"There's no one else here," Melinda said. "Except this asshole."

"Help!" the man screamed.

A mallet swung from the point of view of the camera and struck the man in the chest. He dropped and gasped for breath. Melinda pulled something from the pocket of her hoodie and wrapped it around the man's neck, lifting his face to the camera.

"Smile!" she said.

The man's eyes bulged as he sputtered for breath. Charles recognized him facing frontward: he was Zach Smith, the murder victim that the Parrot had shown him the other day.

Charles' skin grew cold. The video turned off, and Charles moved to turn off the Parrot with a trembling hand.

"I have news for you," the Parrot chimed.

Charles whipped his hand back. The TV flicked on again.

He was less surprised by the images on his screen, but no less horrified. Melinda held another man he'd seen the other day, Dustin Wood; with a cord wrapped around his throat. He had bruises on his skin and blood on his shirt.

"Give him another whack," Melinda said to the person holding the camera. "While he can feel it."

The camera was set down and stayed steady as Melinda's accomplice entered the frame. Charles gripped the couch cushions as Damon walked towards Dustin. He crashed the mallet down on Dustin's leg. Dustin let out a garbled scream.

Charles grabbed his cellphone. He had no clue where Melinda was, but Damon's ass was probably at the mortuary. He'd call the police.

The video cut to the mortuary. Melinda lay on the table as she had when Charles went to see her, when he'd been told she was dead. Her eyes were closed, but there was a smile on her face as she gasped for breath. Damon had his head between her thighs and his twitchy fingers clasped around her hips. Charles' blood boiled as Melinda cried out in ecstasy. Her head lolled to face the camera.

Fuck calling the police. Charles would kill the fucker himself. Charles jumped to his feet, but stopped when a new video began. Melinda sat beside the dead body of another man, presumably the one they'd found in the Potomac River.

"Why'd you kill him?" Damon asked from behind the camera.

Melinda chuckled, then stroked the man's hair. She smiled her sexiest smile, one that in spite of himself, Charles remembered fondly. She looked straight into the camera, making eye contact with him.

"I killed him because I was practicing for you, Charles."

Charles stood frozen.

"I killed him and the others because I want to get it right when we finally come for you."

The video and TV cut off—as did all the lights. The Parrot darkened, then dimmed back on in battery mode. Its green glow was the only light left.

A key turned in the lock, and he heard the front door open. Charles stood still in the dark. Melinda was back. He'd show her. He'd wait in silence on the couch, wait for her to go upstairs or into the kitchen and then take care of her.

The Parrot glowed beside him. "Hello Damon."

Charles' brow furrowed, but before he could turn, he felt something cold and hard smack against his head.

———

Charles opened his eyes and saw blurred shapes. The shapes sharpened into a desk chair, a desk, and Melinda's computer. Her computer stayed off. Damon sat in the chair, thumping his mallet up and down into his palm.

"Hey there, sleepy," he said with a smile.

"Fuck you," Charles growled. He'd been out of it for who knew how long, but he remembered the hellish videos the Parrot had shown him clear as day—especially the way Damon had been eating out his wife.

"I'd rather fuck Melinda."

Charles tried to scramble to his feet, but ended up scooting to no avail. He felt cords wrapped around his wrists.

"Tight little fuckers, aren't they?"

Charles looked up at the sound of Melinda's voice. "Where is she?" he spat.

A cord tightened around his neck. Charles gasped, then coughed. He thrashed and butted his head, until Damon rose and struck him on both ankles. "Thrashing makes it worse," he said.

"Listen to Damon." Melinda crouched in front of Charles. Her hair brushed his cheek as she descended, and she wore the perfume he'd once told her was his least favorite. He'd made his point by dumping it down the toilet. She held two long ends of cord in her hands, and Charles realized that it was the power cord to her computer.

Melinda grinned, then snapped her hands back. Charles flipped onto his back, and his scream was cut short as the cord around his neck tightened.

"I married the wrong man, Charles," she said. "But you married the wrong woman."

A flash of green caught Charles' attention. The Parrot sat on the bookshelf against the wall. "Hello Melinda," it chimed.

"Parrot!" Charles called in a strangled voice, one growing weak in time with both his vision and breath.

"Hello Charles," it chimed.

Damon swung the mallet and struck Charles' chest. The blow felt like a train crashing into his ribs. Charles sputtered and coughed, but managed to choke out, "Parrot, call 911!"

Damon swiveled to face the Parrot with his mallet. "Damon, don't!" Melinda said as she tightened the cord. "It'll be fine."

Charles snorted as his vision blurred. Melinda and her precious tech. She'd been obsessed with her computer all throughout their marriage, and now she was ignoring both Damon and their safety in favor of a damn home device. They were both fools.

"Hello Charles," the Parrot repeated.

"Call 911!" Charles croaked.

"I have news for you."

"Jesus Christ! Call—"

"You're going to die."

Both Melinda and Damon laughed. Charles sagged to the floor as the power cord squeezed out his final breaths.

CANDY

Martha hated Valentine's Day, but she loved the candy. Her favorite was a box of truffles filled with fruit-flavored cream. Every February, when she walked by CVS and saw the sickening display of hearts and teddy bears in the window, her mind would wander to a heart-shaped box filled with truffles, and her mouth would water as she imagined biting into each piece of candy's tender flesh.

When Valentine's Day reared its ugly head again, Martha went straight to the pharmacy, determined to purchase every box of truffles she could find. She walked inside, the white of the tile hurting her eyes. Once she ran her errand, she could retreat to her apartment with her chocolates and only surface for groceries. She kept her eyes on the prize and walked towards the candy aisle.

When she reached the aisle, she was astonished to see how empty it appeared. Candy had been usurped by stuffed Snoopy dolls, plastic roses, and packs of cards that elementary school students could give to their friends. The candy that was there was all wrong: Skittles, M&M's, peanut butter cups that were vaguely shaped like hearts. There were no truffles to be found.

A flash of red came into her periphery. She turned and saw a man in a denim shirt holding one large heart-shaped box. Its cursive letters read, "Truffles."

"Can I have that?" Martha asked.

The man snorted, then walked by her.

"Please," Martha said as she tried to keep her temper down. "They're my favorite."

"My wife's too," he said.

"I came all the way here for those!"

"Find them somewhere else!"

Martha lunged for him, and the man stumbled back. A pharmacy worker who'd overheard her yelling pushed Martha back. "Ma'am, get out of the store before we call security," she said.

Martha swallowed tears and stormed out of the store. She stood outside and tried to collect her breath. All she wanted were those truffles. She'd dreamed of them since she'd run out of her last box from the previous Valentine's Day close to Halloween. How could this stranger do this to her?

The man walked by her as he exited the store. He was on his phone and didn't see her. Martha watched him walk away, then decided to follow him. Maybe she could better plead her case away from nosy pharmacy workers.

The man turned left, and so did Martha. He turned left again, and Martha did as well. He hung up his phone and didn't look back. Martha followed him like a beam of sun through a blind across the floor.

The number of people around them decreased from several to few to zero. When they were alone, Martha quickened her pace to catch up with him. He turned right, and she ran to follow him around the corner.

Martha turned right, and something hard smacked her on the shoulder.

Martha screamed and stumbled to the ground. The man stood over her with a clenched fist. "I knew you'd follow me," he said as he picked her up by her coat. Martha struggled to stay on her feet. "I know how much you like these damn truffles."

"How?" Martha asked.

"Because you bought them all last year!" He threw her against the wall, then held her against the bricks. Martha's head pulsed in pain beneath her hair. "I saw you leaving with a whole cart full of them, and I couldn't get any for my wife. She dumped me, you know that?"

"Over truffles?"

"Shut up!" The man slammed her against the wall again, and she fell in a heap. "You followed me for truffles, don't act all surprised that another woman acted like a crazy bitch over some dumb candy. I hate this damn holiday, and I hate women like you who make it their whole lives."

Martha crawled on the ground and reached into her purse. The man hoisted her up and held her close.

She lifted her can of mace, the one she'd managed to clench before he picked her up, and sprayed it in his face. The man screamed and let her go. Martha punched him once, twice, three times; then kicked him in the balls as he crumpled to the ground. She saw the box of truffles on the ground, and next to it, an abandoned pipe. She picked it up and dealt him one last blow, one that left him barely breathing and bleeding on the bricks.

"I hate Valentine's Day," Martha said. She sat against the wall and opened the box of truffles. She plucked out a piece of dark chocolate with raspberry cream, her favorite. "But I do love Valentine's candy."

THE SHARPS

Camila wrote in her journal by the beam of a flashlight. She wrote in a small cabin on the beach of an abandoned cove, one she'd made plans to stay in all summer to study the marine life in the Foothills River. She was to be isolated—she left her phone back home, left her laptop in her bedroom, packed one last bag to add to the supplies she'd been taking to the cabin throughout the spring, then set sail.

Camila had no idea when she left the mainland that the river would be so willing to aid in her isolation.

On that first day, as her boat entered the cove, she heard rustling in the water. She smiled at the sound, an aquatic hush she'd loved since she was little.

She gazed down at the water, then furrowed her brow. The river was still, and yet the rustling noise continued. It grew louder, and soon, it was accompanied by hissing.

Camila wondered what could be making the noise. There was nothing that hissed in a river in North Carolina; and unless global warming had taken a sharp left turn, she didn't think the river would be boiling. She chuckled to herself, then stopped abruptly when she heard a sharp crunch on the side of her boat.

Camila looked over the side and saw pieces of wood floating into the water. Then a glistening row of fangs leapt from the river.

Camila screamed and jerked back her hand in time to avoid having her fingers bitten clean off. The fangs—and the body that homed them—fell onto the side of the boat and clung to the wood.

Camila jerked to the other side, and saw hundreds of glistening silver bodies swarming the boat. They heaved and groaned beneath the boat, devouring the wood as an appetizer before reaching their desired main course. Camila looked from side to side, desperate for a gap. She reached for her bag, then stopped when she saw whatever creatures had descended upon her boat begin to crawl over the nylon. In a fleeting moment, she reached in, hoping that whatever she had time to grasp would be useful.

Her hand grabbed something small and metal before she jerked it back. A Swiss Army knife. Not the most useful tool against a swarm of ravenous creatures, but it would have to do.

Camila felt a sharp pain in her back, like a thousand yellow jackets combined into one massive stinger that broke through her clothes. She screamed as she grabbed whatever had bitten her and felt velvety, slimy skin, like the back of a sting ray she'd petted as a child. The pain increased a thousand-fold when she yanked the creature from her skin. She threw it back into the water, its teeth stained with her blood. The other creatures swarmed their friend, desperate for a taste.

The swarm created a small gap in the water. Camila ignored the pain in her back as she dove in. She swam faster than she'd ever swam before, moving towards the shore. She heard the hissing begin again behind her—they'd spotted their prey. She had to get to shore. She had to get to the cabin.

Her feet touched the sand, and the water came to lower and lower points on her legs as she ran. She had to stop herself from kissing the ground in relief.

The same sharp pain she'd felt on the boat coursed through her calf. She looked down and saw another creature clinging to her sock. She unfolded the pocketknife, yanked the creature from her leg, then stabbed it through its ravenous head. Its body hung limp on the sand, her blood trickling from its jaws.

Thankfully, the other creatures didn't swarm their fallen brethren for a buffet. They stayed on the edge of the water, hissing and chomping and swarming in circles. Their collective noises sounded like rain upon a stormy beach.

That noise rang in Camila's ears three months later as she wrote in her journal. The tide was high that night, meaning the creatures—which she'd nicknamed the Sharps—were closer to her cabin and swimming in wait. The little fucker that bit her leg sat in a jar of formaldehyde, floating on the window ledge. He'd been a great little tool for sketching and for studying these odd creatures' anatomy. If she left the cove alive, she'd have incredible research to show her department.

With no boat, no phone, no laptop, fewer supplies, and no people, though, leaving the cove alive seemed less likely every day.

Camila was used to falling asleep to the hissing of the Sharps. It was the week of a third quarter moon, and that seemed to be their preferred mating season.

When she opened her eyes the next morning, though, the hissing was still in full swing. Camila was surprised, but her shock was nothing compared to how she felt when a loud knock banged against her door.

Camila tightened into herself in bed. Had the Sharps figured out how to survive outside of water? Were they clamoring against her door, ready to eat their way in?

"Help!"

The Sharps definitely hadn't learned speech. Camila swung her feet to the floor, then stopped. How had anyone found her?

"Please, help m—OW!"

Camila walked towards the door. "Who are you?" she asked.

"My name's Joseph. I was kayaking and—JESUS CHRIST— and something's attacking me, please—"

"Are they behind you?"

"No! Just one on my—FUCK—ankle, please, dear God—"

Camila opened the door. It was barely open a crack before the person on the other side shoved it open and ran inside. He slammed the door behind him, then screamed in pain again. Camila looked down and saw a Sharp gnawing on the man's ankle.

"Hold still," Camila said as she bent down. "And brace yourself."

"Why—OH GOD!" The man cried out as Camila yanked the Sharp from his leg. Blood spilled on the floor. His ankle appeared chewed, but it didn't seem like anything was broken or mangled.

The Sharp—a tiny one, maybe a teenager from a previous mating season—bit at the air between licking Joseph's blood from its teeth. Camila was about to grab her pocketknife when she realized the benefit of having a live creature to study. She dashed to an empty fish tank, dropped the Sharp inside, and slammed the lid down. The Sharp gnawed at the glass, but fortunately couldn't get any traction when it tried to climb up the side of the tank. Camila filled an empty milk jug with water and poured it into the tank, careful to keep the lid as tightly closed as possible in case the Sharp tried to leap from the water.

As Camila filled the jug a second time, Joseph called from behind her, "Um, do you have any Band-Aids?"

Camila's eyes widened as she set down the jug. She turned to face Joseph, who held his wound with increasingly bloody hands. She looked behind her to see if the Sharp had enough water. It swam in its shallow bath and gnashed its teeth. She then turned back to Joseph and ran towards him.

"How do you feel?" she asked as she stooped down next to him.

He looked at her in disbelief. "Shitty."

"No, I mean, does it sting, or does it feel like a deeper wound?"

"It just hurts. I haven't looked at it, I've been trying to stop the blood—"

"Here, just a sec." Camila got her first aid kit, then returned to his side. "This is going to hurt," she said as she wet a cloth with hydrogen peroxide. "But I need to clean it."

"Can't hurt more than the bite." Joseph removed his hands and let Camila take his leg. He screamed when she first touched the rag to his wound, but calmed down as she cleaned it. Thankfully, the Sharp's teeth seemed to merely puncture his skin as opposed to creating a deep cut. Pieces of skin hung from where the Sharp had gnawed away, but no huge chunks were missing.

"I think you'll be alright," Camila said as she continued to clean the wound.

"What if I get a disease or something? Do fish get rabies?"

"Look." Camila leaned back and pulled up the leg of her pajama pants. The scar from the Sharp she kept in the jar glistened on her calf. "I've had this for three months. It hurt like hell before, but I'm okay."

Joseph nodded. He glanced up as Camila returned to cleaning the wound. "Did the little guy in the jar give that to you?"

"Yes." Camila grabbed a piece of gauze.

Joseph smiled at her. "Is that why he's dead in that jar?"

Camila smiled back. "Yes."

Joseph chuckled as Camila wrapped the gauze around his leg. It was a warm sound, one that rang pleasantly in her ears. As the wound became more contained, Camila began to notice Joseph himself. His calf muscle had a nice curve, and felt taut beneath her palm. His dark leg hair was soft against her fingers, and she couldn't help but imagine running her toes along his leg hair while cuddling with him in bed.

Camila blinked away the image. It'd been three months since she'd seen another person—her senses would naturally be on high alert. She looked up and saw Joseph smiling with gratitude. His smile was bordered by a black beard, one that went nicely with his dreadlocks and vibrant brown eyes.

Camila pulled the gauze taut and secured it with first aid tape. "That should stop the bleeding," she said as she stood up. "We can clean it again later."

"Cool." Joseph moved to stand, then winced. Camila held out her hand, and he waved her off. "I've got it," he said.

Camila folded her hands together. She hoped Joseph hadn't seen her staring, and hoped he wasn't uncomfortable with her now.

"Thank you …" Joseph raised his eyebrows. "I don't think you told me your name."

"Camila." She looked towards the kitchen in order to look at anything but him, and saw the teenage Sharp darting back and forth in its shallow bath. She hurried back to the sink and filled another jug with water.

"So, Camila, you said you got the bite on your leg three months ago—do you live here?"

"No." Camila kept her eyes on the Sharp, not wanting to get lost in Joseph's looks again. "I do research here."

"Huh. Nice set-up."

"It belonged to my mother. The marine biology department was able to pay better salaries when she worked for them."

"A family lab on the beach. I can see why you followed in her footsteps."

"It's a good place to work, yes." Camila tapped the glass of the tank, and the teenage Sharp lunged towards her. "At least, it was until these little fuckers showed up."

"Did you come here to study them?"

"Not originally. I come here every summer to study marine life in general. I wasn't counting on these guys." She narrowed her eyes at the Sharp. "I have no idea where they came from. They make no sense. They have arms and legs like small mammals, but gills like fish. They only survive above water for a short time."

"Long enough to keep biting my leg."

"And they mate at … well, an alarming rate. I don't know if they lay eggs or give birth like mammals, but I've heard them once a month since I've been here; and it gets louder with every cycle."

Joseph smiled. "Can't help but think it sucks hearing these assholes get action while you're here alone."

Camila felt a flush creep up her neck. "I don't think about that," she said. It was only a partial lie—she thought about sex, and missed it; but not because the Sharps were breeding loudly every third quarter moon.

"Oh yeah?" Joseph nodded towards her bed. Camila thought he was propositioning her at an alarmingly quick rate, but then she realized he wasn't nodding towards the bed, but her bedside table—which had a large pink dildo resting on top of it.

Camila turned a deep red, and Joseph laughed; but kindly. Desperate to have some sort of dignified upper hand, Camila asked, "Does it bother you that I have that?"

Joseph kept his smile as he arched an eyebrow. "Yes, but not the way you're thinking."

Camila looked back down, but this time with a small smile on her lips. "Well, Sharp mating rituals aside, what bothers me more is not knowing how the hell I'm going to get out of here. They ate my boat, and I'm sure they ate yours too."

"They tried to, anyway."

Camila snapped her gaze up. "Your boat's intact?"

"They were gnawing at it—and me—when I got to shore, but I was so scared I didn't bother looking back."

Camila grabbed her pocketknife and sped towards the door. "Hey, don't go out there!" Joseph called. "A bunch of them were on the boat."

"And they're probably weakened. They stay in the water unless they're stuck on land." Camila ran outside, and screamed with joy when she saw a bright orange kayak on the beach. It was covered with Sharps, but their gnawing was considerably slower. Several hung dead from the sides.

"Jesus!" Joseph approached Camila's side. "They're a lot slower now."

"Because they're dying."

"What about the ones holding out?" Camila pricked her finger with the pocketknife, and Joseph jumped back. "What are—"

"Watch." Camila stooped to pick up an oyster shell, then smeared it with her blood. She clenched her bleeding finger to mask it as best as she could, then approached the kayak. She waved the shell. The living Sharps lifted their heads. Camila tossed the shell further up shore, and the Sharps leapt off the kayak, swarming the shell. Camila dragged the kayak towards the cabin, plucking off dead Sharps and throwing them back in the water. Their corpses didn't last long: marked with her blood, they were easy prey for the more alert Sharps swimming in the water.

Joseph knelt beside her and gingerly touched a dead Sharp. When he was satisfied that it was dead, he plucked it from the kayak and chucked it into the water. Camila examined the kayak as they removed the final Sharps. Not only was it mostly intact—there were several punctures, but they could be patched—but it was a two-seater. A cooler sat in the second seat.

Camila threw her arms around Joseph, careful not to place her bloody finger on his back. Joseph balked in surprise, and Camila loosened her grip. "I'm sorry," she said, "but it's just … you're a miracle."

"No problem." Joseph returned the hug before Camila could release him. She thought she felt him press against her chest a little tighter than a quick hug necessitated, but she was too happy to care. She'd also be lying if she said his chest didn't feel amazing against her own.

They released one another, and Joseph removed the cooler from the kayak. "I have beer in here, if you want to celebrate," he said with a grin as he lifted the lid.

A Sharp leapt up from the cooler, teeth bared. Joseph jumped back, while Camila grabbed the lid and slammed it back over the cooler before the Sharp could fully emerge.

"We'll bring it inside," Camila said as she stood up. "We can put it with the other one."

"Do you know how to tell their sex? The last thing I want is for them to breed."

"Good point. I'll put it in another tank."

———

Camila and Joseph ate peanut butter sandwiches while poring over Camila's notebooks. "This is so much detail," Joseph said as he ran his finger over one of Camila's many diagrams of the dead Sharp she originally retrieved. "You've been studying them all summer?"

"As best as I can. It's too risky to get close to them, but I can watch them swimming and eating. They like to catch birds. Sometimes they cannibalize their own."

"Charming."

"But they've never been as excited as they are about latching onto a human. They almost devoured me alive, and you too. I can't imagine what'll happen if they breed to the point of reaching the public beaches."

"You think they'll get that numerous?"

"They're already reaching past the cove."

"Yeah, that's true. A small group of them smacked against my kayak when I was just outside of the cove, and I made the mistake of turning into there when they all swarmed me."

"What were you doing out here, anyway? It's pretty far out for a row."

Joseph peered at her as he took one last bite. After swallowing, he asked, "You work with Deacon Power?"

"No. I'm a marine biologist."

"I mean, do you work with them at all? Partnerships, reports, stuff like that?"

"They may have funded a grant or two for our department in the past, but I don't work with them directly and they've never funded my work specifically. Why?"

Joseph stayed silent for a moment, then shrugged. "Fuck it. You know Mallard River?"

"Yes. You can get there through a path up the way past the cove's beach."

"Yeah, and through a few other pathways too, further down the river. That's where I was heading. Deacon allegedly had a big waste spill recently."

"Wasn't that a few years ago?"

"That was the one that made the news. They had another one this spring—supposedly." Joseph rolled his eyes in a way that said he didn't believe it was supposed at all.

Camila sighed and also rolled her eyes. "I can't believe it. They're going to destroy that river."

"If they haven't already. I was going there to check out the damage, see what happened to the wildlife."

"What's left of it, anyway. After the last spill, I think the only marine life left was frogs and …"

Camila's eyes widened. Joseph looked at her curiously, but Camila's attention went to the Sharps in their tanks. They swam in circles, hopping from the water but never getting high enough up the glass to make it to the lid. They needed to latch onto something with more traction to stay above water—preferably flesh.

"… and leeches," she said.

———

Joseph huffed behind Camila as they walked through the grasses and dunes that led to a sparse forest. A small path cut through the grass, which Camila used to track their journey. "You know there are leeches in Mallard River," Joseph said between gasps. "Why do you want to check?"

"I want to see just what the damage is like," Camila said. "You do too, right?"

"Right, but not via a ten-mile hike through the marshes." Joseph slapped his shoulder. "Fucking mosquitos."

"It's three miles, and we've only walked about two."

"In a Carolina summer, and again, through marshes."

Camila turned to face Joseph. "I figured you were more outdoorsy."

"I like the water—well, when it isn't full of weird little creatures trying to kill me."

"I have a theory about those little creatures." Camila continued walking down the path, and Joseph followed behind. "One I want to see for—"

Camila skidded to a stop as she entered the woods. Joseph nearly collided into her. "What?" he asked.

"Look," she breathed.

Joseph peered over her shoulder, then gasped. Hundreds of Sharp corpses lay strewn across the mud and the grass. Several lay in heaps at the trunks of trees. Camila wondered if they'd tried to climb up the bark, thinking they'd find food.

"How'd they get all the way out here?" Joseph asked.

"From the river." Camila was certain now.

"Mallard River?"

"Yes. Remember back at the cabin, when I mentioned all I thought had survived from the last spill?"

"I think so. Frogs and leeches."

"Right. Animals that can survive on land for a short while to avoid the sludge." Camila bent down and picked up one of the dead Sharps. "Animals that the latest spill either fused together, or drove from the river after they'd already formed."

"Wait, you think the Sharps are some kind of leech-frog hybrid?"

"I don't know, but they're like nothing I've ever seen before—except in small ways." Camila lifted the Sharp's appendages. "The Sharps have arms and legs, but their fingers and toes aren't as pliable as their teeth. They clasp onto their prey and try to suck them dry. They can jump. They're smooth-skinned, and while they can't survive for long above water, they don't die as quickly as strictly underwater animals."

"Jesus." Joseph looked at the carnage on the path and whistled. "Deacon Power's got a lot of shit to answer for."

"I'm just wondering why these Sharps are littered across the marshes. Unless they were chasing animals, they'd have no reason to leave their home."

"They ended up in the Foothills River."

"Probably from the river basin, yes. But this area's too far away."

"We had a lot of rain this spring. Maybe the river flooded."

Camila's eyes widened, and she almost dropped the Sharp in her hand. She spun around and retraced her path.

"Okay, I'm only going back that way if we're not turning around again to go all the way to Mallard River," Joseph said.

"Look at the grass," Camila said. "Especially on the path."

Joseph looked down. "It's yellow."

"And brown. And dead."

Joseph raised his eyebrows in understanding. He walked back the way they'd come. "And it's like that the rest of the way to the dunes and the cove?"

"Probably. We can check on the way back." Camila smiled. "Yes, we can go back and stay back."

Joseph chuckled, then clucked his tongue as he bent to hold several blades of dead grass in his hands. "Polluted water touched this," he said.

"That's my thought. Maybe the rain flooded the river and sent the Sharps down the path."

"Or maybe Deacon flooded the river when they saw these guys. Clear out the evidence, send them down to an abandoned cove—"

"Or send them on land to drown them, but use so much force that a lucky few made it to the cove, where they're breeding like crazy."

"And getting out into other rivers. They attacked me around the bend from the cove."

"And it's only going to get worse, which is why we need to get back to land." Camila cupped Joseph's elbow and smiled. "Which is why I'm really happy your kayak's intact."

Joseph gave a small smile back. "Well, glad I could help."

"You've helped with more than just the boat. I'll give you a credit in my research paper on these things."

"Sounds good. I'll credit you as a source in my article."

"Article?"

"Yeah. I didn't get to say so back at the cabin, but I'm an environmental reporter. I wanted to check out the Mallard River basin to see what the damage was really like. I suspected it was worse than Deacon was letting on."

Camila cast one last glance back towards the pile of dead Sharps in the marshes. "That's an understatement."

———

Camila and Joseph spent the afternoon patching his kayak as best as they could. Clouds had rolled in as they'd returned to the cabin, and a steady, heavy rain had fallen all afternoon. The rain still sounded against the windows as Camila gathered her notebooks and journals. She wasn't sure how they'd get back for the rest of her research, but she knew most of her things were safer in the cabin than they would be in the boat.

"I'm just not sure how we'll feed these guys while we're gone," Camila said as she dropped a small piece of defrosted raw steak in the tank with the first live Sharp she'd caught. The Sharp rushed towards it and began to suck the meat dry.

"Maybe we should've brought back some of those corpses from the marsh," Joseph said as he flipped the steak he was searing for the two of them. "Let them eat their own."

"Even if they're dead, I'd rather not bring more Sharps in here." Camila dropped the second piece into the second Sharp's tank, then washed her hands and sat down. Joseph brought over the skillet and placed two rare filets on the plates.

"Little weird to not have green beans and mashed potatoes with this," Joseph said with a smile as he sat down to join her.

"We're lucky we had this steak. It's my last piece of frozen meat."

"How much food do you have left?"

"A few pieces of bread, some peanut butter, and a little fruit."

"Jesus. What were you going to do when you ran out of food?"

"I don't want to think about that. I'd rather think about getting out of here."

"Right. So, they sleep, right?" Joseph asked as he jerked a thumb towards the Sharps eating dinner in their tanks. "Because even if they couldn't destroy my boat, they can swarm us without a problem."

Camila took a deep breath as she leaned back against her chair. "The honest answer is, I don't know for sure how we'll get past them."

Joseph shrugged, though disappointment appeared in his eyes.

"But the optimistic answer is, I think we can get out of here by dawn. The Sharps spend almost all night mating. But, in the early morning hours, it's quiet. I think they might be sleeping then. That could be our best chance."

"Dawn. So, an early morning tomorrow."

"Yes. And don't worry, I have an alarm clock."

"Do you have a sleeping bag?"

Camila's eyes widened as she realized Joseph would need a place to sleep. She glanced at the bed, which was a twin. The only other furniture in the cabin was a desk, the table, and chairs.

"I don't," Camila said. "But I'll sleep on the floor."

"Oh, please, you don't need to do that—"

"I insist. Your ankle's hurt, you don't need to sleep on the ground."

"It's not that bad."

"My cabin, my rules." Camila kept a stern expression, and Joseph smiled.

"If you say so," he said.

———

Camila stared into the darkness of the cabin. She couldn't sleep, her set-up on the floor notwithstanding. She listened to the rain outside and watched it run down the windows. She saw the silhouettes of the living Sharps swimming lethargically in their tanks. She hoped they slept at the same time as their free brethren—maybe their stillness would give her a precise time to wake up Joseph and escape from the cove.

What would she have done if Joseph hadn't arrived? She knew her food was getting low, and that the day she was supposed to boat home had passed. She knew her generator wouldn't last much past summer. She'd known all those things, but still passed the days doing research on the Sharps and hoping to make a season's worth of lemonade out of the biggest heap of lemons she'd ever received.

As she lay awake that night, though, it struck her that her only endgame had been to die. She would've died in the cabin if someone hadn't come to help. The closest building was at least twenty or thirty miles away, and that was a lucky guesstimate. Her department may have sent someone to the cabin, but how would they get past the Sharps? Joseph had been lucky. She hoped that luck would continue for both of them when they tried to escape.

It was an escape she hadn't even considered when she felt she was trapped. She'd been so wrapped up in hoping for the best, that she'd done nothing to ensure her safety when her own luck ran out. How could she have made such a terrible error? How could she have left so many ways to ask for help back on land? Her extensive research on the Sharps was all for naught if she had no way to get it back to her department. Camila felt her cheeks grow hot as her throat tightened around a growing lump. She felt like a fool.

"Are you awake?" Joseph asked.

Camila pressed her lips together. She didn't want Joseph to hear her cry. She swallowed, then whispered, "Yes."

"What's wrong?" he asked.

Even her whisper couldn't mask her pain. "I … I was just thinking about what I would've done if you hadn't arrived," she said. "I didn't make a plan—"

"Can't blame you, with those things swimming around in the cove."

"But I was here for three months, studying them and writing notes and I … I honestly didn't know what I was going to do. My boat was destroyed, and I'm God knows how far away from any people or buildings, and because I'm so dedicated to being off the grid to do my studies, I left my phone at home and don't have wi-fi here, and ..."

Camila wiped away tears from her cheeks. She swallowed again, then took a deep breath. She was so desperate not to cry, but with every effort not to, the urge to do so grew greater.

"Camila, you can ... I swear I'm just being nice, I'm not trying to hit on you, but you can come up here if you want."

Camila gulped back another cry, and she heard the mattress squeak beneath Joseph moving. "I'll even sit up," he said. "Nothing sketchy, really. But you don't have to stay on the floor."

Camila stood up and saw Joseph looking at her with pity. She sat next to him, then fell against his shoulder. She wrapped her arms around his waist and cried into the sleeve of his undershirt. Joseph held her tightly.

"It was my fault I got stuck here," she said.

"No it wasn't," he whispered. "You weren't counting on those things to show up."

"I just feel like an idiot, like I did this to myself."

"Hey, I left my own phone back in the car because I didn't want it to get ruined. It's not like I came here prepared for anything. I'd be trapped and bleeding on the sand if you weren't here to help me out."

"I didn't have a plan. I figured the Sharps would miraculously disappear and I could try to swim, or build a raft from some logs, or something. But they didn't. They kept breeding and they kept staying put, and when they didn't leave, I figured I'd just stay here until ... until my food ran out, or the generator died, and then—"

85

"That's not happening." Joseph held her close and rubbed her back. It felt so good to be comforted, to know she wasn't alone anymore; and that she maybe had a chance against the ravenous creatures.

"You're not going to die here," he said. "Those little bastards have another thing coming."

"I hope so," Camila said.

"I know so." Joseph pulled away, then wiped her remaining tears from her cheeks. "You've done nothing but be the smartest person in the room. I trust you to get us out of here. That's more than I can say for myself."

Camila smiled, then pulled Joseph in for another hug. He held her close and rocked her. She wanted to kiss him. She wanted to run her hands beneath his undershirt and feel the hairs she saw peeking out from his collar. She wanted to undress him and explore every inch of his body with her hands and her tongue.

Joseph moved his hands from her face, but before he could put them down by his side, Camila took one. She turned his hand over and began to run her fingertips along the lines of his palm. Joseph looked down. While he stayed silent, he also didn't move his hand.

"Thank you for being so kind," she said.

Joseph brushed a few strands of Camila's hair back behind her ear. "You deserve it. You … I know I've only known you for a day, but you're one of the smartest women I've ever met; and one of the nicest to boot. You're wonderful."

The warmth between Camila's legs pulsed a little harder with every word Joseph said. His fingers traced down from behind her ear to her neck. He was so close to her. He wasn't nearly as close as she would've liked.

Camila released his hand. Joseph furrowed his brow. "Bad timing?" he whispered.

"No," Camila said as she cupped his face. Joseph placed both hands on her waist as she pulled him close and kissed him.

Joseph and Camila melted into a slow enjoyment of one another. Joseph kissed Camila on her lips, her eyebrows, her ears, and her neck. Camila rolled his shirt over his head, then ran her lips and tongue across his chest.

"We can just see where this goes," Joseph whispered as his fingers moved down her sides. "But I want you so much."

Camila gently lay Joseph down across the bed . "I want you too," she said as she removed her top. "All of you."

Joseph smiled as Camila lay down next to him. They kissed on their sides before Camila moved onto her back. He lowered himself over her. His kisses moved from one breast to the other, to her stomach. His fingers moved to the band of her pajama shorts, which he pulled down as he kissed her hips. Camila sighed and stared up at the ceiling. The sound of rain outside the cabin along with their breathing made for the greatest sounds she'd heard in weeks.

Afterward, they lay naked in bed, spooning as best as they could in the twin bed. The rain had become a shush that lingered outside the window. "Hope this rain lets up before our grand escape," Joseph said.

"Me too," Camila said. She coughed a little, her throat dry from the great work Joseph had done to make her scream. She got out of bed to get a glass of water. "The last thing we need is to get …"

She looked out the window with wide eyes.

"… drenched," she finished, but it sounded like an afterthought.

"What is it?" Joseph asked. "Can you see something through the rain?"

Camila stood to the side and pointed to the window. The window was dry, and the sky was clear. "It's not raining anymore," she said.

Joseph furrowed his brow. "Then how come I can hear it raining? It sounds like a million drops banging against the water."

"It's the Sharps."

Joseph's eyes widened. "What?"

Camila peered out the window. A Sharp crashed against the glass, its teeth gnashing at the cracks. Camila screamed and jumped back.

"It's the cove!" Camila shouted over their hissing as she moved away from the window. "It's flooded from all the rain!"

The window cracked again. More Sharps thrashed against the glass. Camila stood on tiptoe and saw that the beach was entirely flooded with water. Sharps swam and jumped in swarms around the cabin.

"Can they get in here?" Joseph asked.

"Eventually. They'll either break the glass or chew through the wood."

"How do we get out?"

"I don't know! I …" Camila looked around the cabin, desperate for some kind of inspiration. The captive Sharps swam in their tanks, smashing their heads against the glass. The dead one floated in its jar, oblivious. Other items lay strewn about the cabin that were all of little use: jars, notebooks, food. If only she had some sort of glass bubble they could wear, or—

"Wait!" Camila dove towards a box under the table, then pulled out several packets of ponchos. "Put these on after you get dressed," Camila said as she tossed several bags to Joseph.

"What? They'll tear these to shreds!"

"They're durable, and if we put on all of them, maybe we can get far enough away before they tear through. It's our best chance."

"What about the parts the ponchos don't cover?"

"Joseph, if we try to leave with the ponchos on, we might die. But if we stay here, we'll definitely die. We have to try."

Joseph nodded and pulled on his underwear. They got dressed, and Camila hastily threw her notebooks and the dead Sharp in the jar into the cooler. She and Joseph then put on as many ponchos as they could fit over their bodies. She could barely put her arms down, but she was fairly certain it would take far too long for any Sharps to reach her skin.

"Okay. How do we do this?" Joseph asked.

"Let's get the kayak near the door. Then, you open it, and we duck. Start rowing once the water flows in. Keep your head down and just get the fuck away from those creatures."

"Got it. But … well, they're probably going to destroy all of your stuff. If they don't, the water will."

Camila looked around the cabin one last time. Only a few of her notebooks were able to fit in with the dead Sharp in the cooler. Out of all three months of research, only about three weeks' worth would be coming with her.

Her research wouldn't do her any good, though, if she died along with it in the cabin. "I have enough notes to start my paper," she said. "And enough memories to finish it—so long as we get out of here."

Joseph nodded. "I'll do my best to get us both out."

Camila nodded, then sat in the back seat of the kayak. She held the cooler between her legs and held her pocketknife in her hand. Joseph stepped into the kayak, took a deep breath, then opened the door.

The hissing surged in Camila's ears as water poured into the cabin. It rushed over the sides of the kayak. Camila gasped as several Sharps landed on the side, and she feared they'd be swarmed before they could float. The kayak, though, lifted upward. They surged out the door almost immediately, Joseph's paddle moving quickly through the current.

Camila stabbed a Sharp that crawled towards her knees. It began to bleed, and other Sharps on the kayak swarmed it. She brushed them into the water with her arm.

The relief was short. The flooded cove was filled with gleaming, swimming, hungry Sharps. They dove on Camila and Joseph. She heard their gnashing against the plastic of the ponchos. "Fuck!" Joseph yelled; but the boat continued to move forward.

A Sharp slid onto Camila's legs. She grabbed it and stabbed it in one fell swoop. She tossed it into the water, then felt a lightness on her back as several Sharps dove in after it. Still more in the water swarmed the growing pool of blood, clearing a small path for their boat.

"Keep rowing!" Camila shouted over the hissing.

"I'm trying!" Joseph shouted back.

"I can help!" Camila looked up, praying that there weren't any Sharps hiding on the hood of the poncho ready to swarm her face. She saw several Sharps on Joseph's back, tearing away at the ponchos. They hadn't reached his skin, but they were close.

Camila yanked one from his back, stabbed it, and tossed it into the water. The living Sharps behaved as they'd done before, ready to eat their own if it meant finally feasting on blood. More space cleared in the path ahead of them.

"Go as fast as you can!" Camila yelled, though it was of little use. Joseph was already rowing manically through the growing swarms of Sharps. Camila grabbed another Sharp off his back, then another. She tossed their corpses in the river, and their friends devoured them whole.

"It's clear up ahead!" Joseph cried.

Camila looked up. The water stood still around the bend from the cove. She looked behind her, and saw Sharps swimming around blooming bloody circles where she'd tossed the creatures' bodies.

"Keep going!" Camila said. "I'll—OW!"

Camila felt a sharp pain in her shoulder. She grabbed until she felt an engorged body in her palm. She yanked it up. Its head snagged on the frayed edges of her chewed-up poncho.

The Sharp lunged back down to her shoulder and bit her again. Camila screamed, and Joseph looked back.

"Don't look at me," Camila pleaded. "Keep rowing!"

"Jesus! That Sharp is gigantic!"

"Just get us out of here!"

Joseph turned around and continued to row. Camila took a deep breath, then pulled off the ponchos covering over her body. She spun up the gigantic Sharp like a spider weaving a fly, then gave one final yank.

The Sharp broke free from her shoulder, and a splurt of blood shot from its mouth. Camila cried out in pain, then in anger as she flung the engorged Sharp into the river. The closest Sharps swarmed it, some even abandoning the smaller corpses they'd been feasting on before.

Their glimmering bodies darkened and their hissing quieted as the scene moved further and further behind them. Camila held her shoulder and turned to watch as Joseph rowed as quickly as possible. They'd gotten away. They'd made it out of the cove.

———————

Joseph and Camila rowed the rest of the way in silence. Camila didn't want to break the spell of their escape until her feet were on land. She assumed Joseph felt the same. The moon glowed over the water, and the only sound beside them was the loll of gentle currents against the kayak.

Joseph veered left. Camila looked up and saw the shore. Behind it was a silver pickup truck—she presumed it was Joseph's—and her own van. She clasped her hand over her mouth and felt tears of relief sting her eyes. They were back. They'd made it.

Joseph rowed to shore, then hopped out of the kayak and pulled it up on the beach. He smiled at Camila as he helped her out of the kayak. "How's your shoulder?" he asked as he gently touched her upper arm.

"Sore." Camila ran her fingers over the wound. Her shirt felt mucked with blood, but it seemed to be drying; indicating that the wound was healing. "I don't think the Sharp got too much blood out of me."

"Still, we should clean it." Joseph ran to his truck and unlocked the door. Camila felt a flash of panic, then felt her pockets. They were empty.

"Shit!" she hissed.

"What?" Joseph asked as he trotted back, a first aid kit in hand.

"I left my keys back at the cabin. Just great—the Sharps got most of my research, my car, *and* my apartment."

Joseph chuckled as he poured hydrogen peroxide on some gauze. "Well, at least they didn't get you," he said as he pressed the cloth to her wound.

Camila winced at the pain, but only a little. She calmed as she looked into Joseph's eyes. He cleaned her wound, then taped a fresh piece of gauze over it. "That should keep it clean," he said as he gave her shoulder one last, gentle pat.

"Thank you," Camila said.

"Of course. You did the same for my ankle."

"And … and thank you so much for getting us out of there."

Joseph smiled, then pulled her close. "You cleared a path through the Sharps by getting them to eat themselves. I never would've gotten past the cabin without that."

Camila hugged him, then gave him a kiss. Joseph held her close and kept his lips pressed to hers. One kiss became two. She knew there would be several more.

"Let's not leave quite yet," she whispered.

———

The cooler with the specimen sat in the front seat of Joseph's truck. The truck still sat next to Camila's van near the shore. The night was warm and full of stars. The only sounds around them were crickets, toads, and the water.

More sounds, though, came from the bed of Joseph's truck. Both Joseph and Camila were too impatient to drive to a motel. They paused only for Joseph to lay a couple blankets across the metal floor.

The croaking of frogs and the singing of crickets whirred together like a hum. The hum became a buzzing, one that soon began to sound like rain upon the water.

Camila's heart began to race. She looked to the side as Joseph kissed her neck.

She saw trees. She heard no water. The sounds of nature swirled in Camila's ears as she relaxed into Joseph's hold. They were only the songs of creatures enjoying the night. She and Joseph were out of the water. They were safe.

YOU PROMISED ME FOREVER

Cody was being so gentle tonight. His fingertips grazed Carrie's body as if she were made of fine linen. Carrie relished his touch, enjoyed the feel of his hips between her legs; but wished he'd be more aggressive. "I'm not a porcelain doll," she whispered in his ear before biting his ear lobe.

Cody gasped with pleasure, then bent to kiss her neck. "I want to feel your skin," he said with his lips still pressed against her body. "While it's still warm."

"I'll always be warm for you," Carrie said through a moan that escaped her lips.

Cody lifted his head and looked into her eyes. "Will you always say such cheesy things in bed?"

"You love it," Carrie said with a smile as she playfully batted Cody's shoulder. She ran her fingertips over his lips. "You feel warm."

"It's a different kind of warm."

"As long as it's warmth for me."

"It is." Cody bent back down and kissed Carrie's shoulder. "It always will be."

His lips grew hot, and his mouth spread wider. Carrie closed her eyes and gripped his back as she felt the edges of his teeth graze her neck. "Forever?" she asked, though she already knew the answer.

The pain from his fangs was sudden and swift. Carrie cried out, but didn't lose her smile. She wrapped her legs around Cody's waist as he suckled the nape of her neck, her favorite place to be kissed. He lifted his head and Carrie fell back on the pillow, delirious with lust and a bit from blood loss. He grinned through her blood smeared over his face as he lifted a pen knife toward his wrist.

"Forever."

————

Carrie's feet skid across the linoleum floor. She let out an angry sigh as she turned towards the living room. "Cody!"

Cody glanced at her from the couch, then turned back to the TV. Whether or not he saw her angry glare, Carrie couldn't say. He almost never seemed interested in looking at her longer than necessary. "What?" he asked.

"I almost fell and killed myself on the blood on the floor. Again."

"You can't get killed that way, you're a vampire."

"You know what I mean!"

Cody stayed silent. Carrie crossed her arms. "Can you at least clean it up?"

"Yeah."

Carrie continued towards the fridge and looked inside. There were several cups of blood, enough that they wouldn't need to hunt again for a couple weeks. She felt a gnawing disappointment—not at the abundance of food, but for not being able to do the one thing they seemed to actually want to do together lately.

Carrie remembered when they first met, when she was still human and didn't know what Cody was beyond a handsome man. They danced in a bar, then fucked in her apartment. The only thing she noticed about him was that while his lips and his tongue ran all over her skin, he was careful not to bite her.

As they got to know each other, revealing more and more about their lives, Carrie noticed that while Cody always had an answer for her questions—what did he do, where had he grown up—his eyes would seem further and further distressed when he answered them. One evening, as they held hands in the park and watched the moon and stars glitter on the surface of a lake, Cody pressed his cheek into Carrie's hair and said, "I need to tell you something."

"What?"

"It's something I've wanted to tell you for a while now, but—"

Carrie turned to face Cody and said, "You can tell me anything you want. It won't change a thing."

"I would hope so. I'd really hope that, actually, because …" Cody swallowed, and Carrie smiled.

"I love you too," she said.

Cody's eyes widened, and he chuckled a little. Carrie felt a tiny rush of panic. "And if that wasn't what you were going to say," she continued, "then let's leave it at 'I love you,' because I do—"

"I do love you, Carrie."

"—and I think I will forever."

Cody smiled. "You only think?"

Carrie laughed a little. "I mean, I'd like to think I know, but I know forever is a long time."

"Few know that more than I do. That's what I wanted to talk to you about."

Carrie furrowed her brow. "About forever?"

"Sort of. It's …" Cody sighed, then said, "Fuck it. I should show you. But I want you to know that you were never in danger."

Carrie kept her smile, but worried a little at his words. "Danger? What are you—"

She stopped when Cody parted his lips. She saw two fangs finish their descent from his gums.

Several thoughts began to pulse through her brain in time with her heartbeat rising. How long had he had fangs? Was she seriously involved in a vampire romance? Vampires were real? What did this mean for them? But with everything she felt, she felt very little fear; because around those fangs she only saw Cody's face.

———

Carrie huffed as she grabbed a cup of blood from the fridge. Cody stayed seated on the couch, despite his promise to clean up the floor. She stewed with each minute that passed and Cody remained still.

Cody reached for her cup as he kept his eyes on the TV. "Thanks," he said.

Carrie looked at him in disgusted shock. "This isn't for you," she said. "Don't just assume I'm bringing you food."

"Okay, can you please get me some?"

The snide way he asked annoyed her more than his assumption. "Maybe after you clean up from your last meal."

He finally turned to face her. "I said I'd clean it."

"When? Sometime this week?"

"I'll do it tonight."

"Do it now!"

"Fine! Just say that next time!"

Cody got up and Carrie closed her eyes. When she'd agreed to be transformed, to live forever with Cody, she hadn't thought they'd still argue and snap at each other like every other old married couple.

She'd been careful, so careful. She'd considered her options in the context of Cody, not some lovestruck girl who thought vampires were romantic or that becoming a vampire meant an unbreakable bond. Vampires hadn't meant much to Carrie at all before Cody. Sure, she enjoyed the occasional vampire story, and entertained the notion of how she'd escape from one if they were real. But Cody meant the world to her, and as they spoke of staying together, Carrie wanted to consider what that meant for them both.

"It's not as easy as just living forever," Cody had said as they walked in their favorite park, the same one where he'd first revealed his fangs to her.

"I know about the sun," Carrie had replied, somewhat jokingly. "And I've never liked garlic."

"It's more than the stereotypes."

"Wait, can you be out in the sun?"

"Not without a hat, but that's not the point." Cody had kept his serious expression, and Carrie had known to stop joking. "It's about what it means to everyone around you. Not everyone you know will become a vampire. You're going to watch your friends, your parents, everyone around you age and then die; while you stay stuck the way you were before you turned. Is that something you want?"

Carrie had held his cheek, looked in his eyes, and said without missing a beat, "If it means you don't have to watch me do the same, then yes."

Now, though, as she watched Cody huff and roll his eyes while he grabbed a paper towel, Carrie wasn't so sure.

––––––––

Carrie swallowed her last bit of blood as Cody threw away the last paper towel. They'd both been silent the whole time he'd cleaned up the mess, and Carrie knew the last thing she wanted was to be next to Cody. She got up as he moved towards the living room and kept her eyes on the door. "I'm going out," she said as she grabbed her purse.

Cody didn't say anything. He simply sat back down on the couch with a huff. Carrie debated saying "I love you" as she opened the door. She said it almost every time they parted. She never wanted her last words to him to be something different.

Tonight, though, she didn't feel that sense of regret for a parting that hadn't yet happened. Instead, when she thought of being away from him, she felt better. Her heart broke a little as the truth of her feelings settled into her skin. She walked out the door in silence. It wasn't lost on her that Cody hadn't said a word to her before she left.

––––––––

Carrie walked along the mostly empty streets and pulled out her phone. There weren't many friends she'd been able to see since she turned—as Cody told her, she could wear a hat in daylight, but she still felt its burn through her clothes if she stayed out too long—but there was one she could count on, so long as she was on break. *Can I come see you?* she texted.

She continued on her route, one that included the park she and Cody had spent so much time in. After her transformation, they hunted there, waiting for the inevitable person who chose to walk alone through the park's darkest corners.

The first time Carrie had snatched a living person, her guilt at the attack was assuaged by how invigorated she felt when she tasted his blood as his heart pumped out food. "You'll want to completely drain him," Cody instructed as she drank. "We can't have him coming to and remembering anything—or worse, turning without another vampire to help him."

"I know," Carrie said after swallowing a gulp of blood. She felt a flash of irritation, one that Cody noticed.

"What?" he'd asked.

"Nothing."

"Forever's going to be a long time if we're not honest with each other."

"Just … don't treat me like I'm stupid. I heard you the first time."

"I only told you once."

"You told me before we even got to the park."

"Well, it's important."

"Just have some faith in me, okay?"

"Okay."

And he had, though it took a few more hunting trips before he stopped trying to be her mentor instead of her partner. Now though, he was simply there—whether Carrie wanted him to be or not. She pursed her lips as she looked at the park's empty benches. A small lump burned in her throat, but no tears came. One of the things she was surprised to lose when she turned were her tears—no need for tear ducts if she were technically dead, she supposed. She wished, though, that her transformation had been kind enough to consider deleting the emotions that tears eased if she had no way to soothe them.

When Carrie first had turned, it didn't bother her as much to lose so much because in return, she had Cody. Cody would be her company when she couldn't see her family or friends. Cody would be there when she looked into forever and saw the gaping threat of loneliness. How would she face that threat, though, if she didn't feel soothed by going through it with Cody?

Carrie's throat burned fiercely, and she was about to release a scream into the starry sky. She may not have been able to cry, but she could still shout and yell—something Cody was all too familiar with. She smirked a little, then smiled more when her phone chimed with a message: *Sure, I'll take a break in 10.* She wasn't entirely alone without Cody—not yet.

———

"Carrie!"

Marliese bounded across the lobby, her smile as bright as her fuchsia scrubs. Carrie held out her arms and felt her skin warm—as best as it could, anyway—as she and Marliese shared a hug. She smelled Marliese's familiar combination of hairspray and Beyond Paradise perfume, and as she'd grown accustomed to since her transformation, had to temper her stomach at the scent of Marliese's blood pulsing through her veins.

"You aren't hungry, are you?" Marliese said with a smile.

"No," Carrie said, "I ate before I got here."

Marliese raised her eyebrows, and Carrie added, "It was from the fridge."

"I still don't need to know where you got it." Marliese motioned her towards the hospital cafeteria. "Come on, I don't have too long a break."

"I hope I'm not interrupting anything—"

"No, it's good for now! I just finished my rounds." Marliese squeezed Carrie's elbow as they entered the cafeteria. Marliese was Carrie's only friend that knew she'd been transformed.

Marliese, like Carrie when she learned the truth about Cody, had been more shocked at the existence of vampires than the fact that someone she knew had become one. She'd asked Carrie if she knew what she was doing. She asked if Cody was really worth how much she'd lose. Carrie said yes, and Marliese believed her. Carrie sometimes wished her friend had maybe had a little less faith in her.

They sat with two cups of coffee at an isolated table, Carrie's cup more for appearances than actual consumption. "So," Marliese said as she added sugar to her cup. "What's got you texting me at one in the morning?"

Carrie sighed as she traced the rim of her coffee cup. "It's Cody. Well, it's me and Cody."

"Trouble in gothic paradise?"

"I'm serious, Marliese."

Marliese made a zipping motion across her lips, apology in her eyes. Carrie continued, "Things are weird between us. It seems like whenever we're in the same room, we tolerate each other at best. When we started dating, there was so much passion, so much heat. I didn't want to ever be apart from him."

"Obviously not, given you wanted to live forever along with him."

"But that's the problem: I don't know if I want to do that anymore. It's more than just little things here and there. It's like we're in each other's way instead of together. It's like he takes me for granted, and expects me to be his minder or his nanny."

Marliese snorted. "Sounds like most men."

"But I thought he'd be different."

"Why, because he has fangs? Vampire men are still men— and shit, that's something I never thought I'd say with a straight face."

"I know he's still a man."

"Then why's it such a shock to you that he's acting like one?"

"I don't think it's that shocking to expect better from him." Carrie swallowed and brushed her eyes, even though there weren't any tears. "I didn't think it'd be that outrageous to think we wouldn't get bored with each other, that we wouldn't turn into a happily ever after that peters out the moment there's work to be done or we disagree on something. I didn't think we'd be—"

"Human?"

Carrie's shoulders dropped, and Marliese looked at her with pity. "Look," Marliese said. "I'm not going to pretend to be an expert on vampires versus humans, especially with their relationship drama. But couples get bored sometimes, or get into ruts, or fight a lot. It happens. It doesn't mean it's forever."

"It feels like forever, though. And if this is what forever with Cody means, especially if it means literally, actually forever, then I don't know if I can take it."

Carrie sipped her coffee on instinct, then gagged. It tasted like rancid mud. "Jesus," she said as she spat the coffee back into her cup. "You know what I'd give to have some of what I had before again? Like being able to taste something other than blood and not gag—"

"Whoa, quiet down a little," Marliese said as she waved her hand.

"Or to be able to cry? Vampires can't do that. We're dead everywhere except our brains, and our stomachs. I thought that Cody would be enough to fill those voids, would be enough for me, but ..." Carrie trailed off, not wanting to repeat herself and bore her friend.

Marliese looked at Carrie in silence, pity in her eyes. She drummed her nails on the table, and Carrie wondered what she was contemplating.

"What do you think I should do?" Carrie asked.

Marliese waited a few moments, then leaned forward. In a low voice, she asked, "Do you really not want this life anymore?"

"I ... I don't know. Why?"

Marliese looked around, then stood up and beckoned Carrie to follow. "You have to promise not to say a word."

————

Carrie waited outside the outpatient pharmacy on a vinyl couch. She wondered what Marliese wanted to show her that was such a big secret. As she waited, other doctors and nurses walked by. The hospital was quieter at night than during the day, but there was still a flurry of human activity that her senses couldn't help but detect. She may have no longer had a heartbeat, but she could hear another person's pulse from several feet away. The scent of their blood would come next, causing her to lick her lips, though only in memory of salivation. She bit her lip—carefully, given her fangs—as an especially sumptuous nurse walked by. It didn't help that he was also handsome, awakening other senses within her.

She wondered if Cody had been hungry for her in another way before she offered to buy him a drink at the bar. When he'd first told her he was a vampire, he'd promised her that he'd never considered her to be potential prey. He'd only ever wanted to fuck her, date her, then love her. She wondered how true that was, at least when she was still a stranger to him. She wondered further if he'd regain interest if he could smell her blood once more.

"Hey."

Marliese sat down beside Carrie as soon as Carrie heard her speak. Marliese leaned close to her, shoulder-to-shoulder. She moved her hand to Carrie's. Carrie opened her hand and Marliese squeezed two small vials into her palm.

"What're these?"

Marliese closed Carrie's fingers over the vials. "Put them in your purse," she said. "And keep your voice down."

"What if I don't need them?"

"Then give them back later. Please, just put them in your purse." Marliese looked so worried that Carrie relented. She tucked the vials below her wallet. She saw a deep crimson color before she zipped up her purse.

"So ... are you going to tell me about what I may or may not take, or do I just need to risk it?" Carrie smiled even though she was serious. Marliese gave a small smile back, then lowered her face close to Carrie's ear so she could speak quietly.

"So, you know how I pretty much believed you about being a vampire, even before you showed me your fangs and all that, when anyone else would've thought you were high?" Marliese asked.

"Yeah?"

"You weren't the first person to talk to me about vampires. We'd get patients that had weird bite marks and blood loss. They'd have insomnia, but would scream if daylight touched them. They'd refuse their food, saying it tasted nasty—nastier than typical hospital food."

It all sounded like Carrie's first days in Cody's care after her transformation. She hugged herself, remembering how Cody had held her and told her she would get used to it, and to not worry because he was there. She closed her eyes at the memory of his nurturing touch.

"Well, Dr. Gorman started thinking it wasn't some weird, inexplicable disease," Marliese continued. "He knew it sounded crazy, but everything about their behavior suggested they'd been bitten but not completely drained."

"Whoever bit them was being sloppy. They should've been drained." Marliese shuddered a little, and Carrie waved her hand to prompt Marliese to continue.

"Dr. Gorman started talking to the victims without any other nurses, asking them to describe what happened. They all said they remembered being bitten, and several said they felt like vampires. Hating food, craving blood, avoiding the sunlight—I mean, come on, that's what we all think. But we also all think it's fake. Or thought, anyway. But we all know what makes a vampire, and we also all know what ..."

Marliese trailed off, and Carrie furrowed her brow.

Marliese continued, more carefully, "Dr. Gorman took what they were telling him about their bodies. They talked about needing blood to eat. He noticed when they'd sip it, they'd get a flush and feel a little warmer, and also that their veins would appear while they were full. But when he'd examine them, they'd have no heartbeat."

"Yeah. We're dead."

"So he thought, what if he could give them medicine that seeps blood into their veins while also jump-starting their heart? The heart would beat, the missing piece to keep that blood flowing throughout the body, as opposed to dissipating or going stagnant or whatever it is that happens when you all get hungry again." Marliese gestured to Carrie's purse. "Those pills are concentrated capsules made from blood cells, and also trigger the heart's synapses. You take it right after a meal. It may take two or even three, but once the heart starts going, it doesn't stop. It's worked wonders for a ton of his patients."

"Jesus. It focuses on the heart? It almost sounds like a stake." Carrie was joking that time, but her smile faded when Marliese looked down in shame. "Why do you keep looking embarrassed?"

"Because what I was going to say before, about all of us knowing about vampires? He says that also means we all know how to kill them."

Carrie froze. "Does this … does it kill vampires?"

"I wouldn't give it to you if I didn't think it was safe."

"Then why give it to me at all? It may not kill me, but it'll kill a part of me."

"Because if the only reason you're staying with Cody is because you're both vampires, then you have a way out of that. You said the idea of being a vampire was only made better when you were in love with Cody."

"I'm still in love with Cody. Well … I think so, anyway …"

"And it's okay to not be sure. We're never sure about forever, even though we say it to the people we love all the time. Even being a vampire isn't a guarantee. What if someone stakes Cody while he's out? What if some vampire council decides you're breaking the rules and snaps your heads?"

"There's no vampire council."

"Well, whatever! And what if Cody falls out of love with you?"

Carrie sat in silence, eyes wide.

"You keep saying you don't know what to do. 'Cody's why I'm a vampire, I can't leave Cody,'" Marliese said, her eyes filled with warmth and pity. "What if Cody leaves *you*? What if he feels the same way you do but actually takes the next step and leaves? Do you really want to spend forever with a broken heart?"

Carrie didn't know the answer. She looked down at her purse again, and swallowed despite no tears.

"You don't have to take the medicine if you don't want to," Marliese said as she laid a hand on Carrie's shoulder. "But you chose to be a vampire. You should be able to choose to go back to the way you were. It's only fair."

Carrie nodded, even though she wasn't sure she agreed. She didn't know how she felt. "How did you know all this?" she asked. "About Dr. Gorman, I mean?"

"I knew he had thoughts on what was happening to these patients, but when you told me you had a vampire boyfriend and planned to join him, and I subsequently saw you, a vampire, with my own eyes …" Marliese shrugged. "I figured he needed a nurse. And I knew he needed someone who believed him."

"And these aren't meant to kill vampires."

"No. They're meant to transform you back into a human. One with a pulse, one who can taste food and be in the sun and cry when you're sad."

Carrie thought of everything she missed about being human. She wondered if she missed it enough to leave Cody behind.

"I have to get back to my rounds," Marliese said. They both stood up and hugged each other goodbye. Marliese held Carrie a little tighter, and said, "Just think about it, okay?"

Carrie nodded against Marliese's shoulder. They broke apart, and Marliese returned to her rounds. Carrie left the hospital, unable to ignore the sound of the pills rattling in her purse.

The first time Carrie had considered she'd made the wrong choice was about six months after she'd turned. She and Cody had fallen into a pattern of hunting, gathering blood, and avoiding daylight. It also dawned on her how lonely an existence being a vampire could be. She and Cody had each other, but they only had each other. She avoided her family so she could avoid their questions or their curious glances. Most of her friends, save for Marliese, had accepted her disappearance with a readiness Carrie was almost offended by. "That's life when you're not single anymore," they'd joked, as if they knew Carrie would inevitably give all of herself to someone and never be heard from again—and worse, that they would be okay with that.

When those nagging feelings crept up on her, she'd brush them away by telling herself it would feel worse to not be with Cody. But six months in, she found she wasn't as easily able to brush them away as she had before. Her throat began to tighten. Carrie waited for the tears to fall. They never came. But the tightness never left. She felt the urge to cry but didn't have the means to do it. She began to choke out dry sobs, punctuated by gasps.

"Carrie?"

Cody stood in the bedroom doorway, watching her. "What's wrong?" he asked.

How could she tell him that the life he'd warned her about, the life she'd agreed to start with him, was making her upset? She didn't want him to think she didn't want to be with him. Far from it. She simply wished there was a way they could be with each other, be like each other, without feeling the crushing loneliness of being unable to feel anything without borrowing another's warmth through their blood.

"I can't believe I'm saying this," Carrie said, "but … I miss being able to cry."

Cody stared at her in pity, then left the doorway. A loud sob escaped Carrie's throat, one that seemed to punch her with its dryness. Cody didn't understand. Cody wouldn't understand. Carrie was truly alone.

Cody returned with a glass of water and a small Styrofoam cup, one that Carrie knew held blood. "I'm not hungry," Carrie said.

"This isn't for food." Cody sat beside her, then poured a small amount of blood into the glass of water. "This will make the water palatable."

"I don't need water."

"But you need to cry." He held the glass towards her. Carrie took it, then sipped. The water was faintly rancid on her tongue, but the blood did help. What helped more was feeling the water coat her throat, and in turn, the slightest brimming of tears in her eyes. She drank the rest of the glass. The lump in her throat cracked, and a tear rolled down her cheek.

Carrie buried her face into Cody's shoulder and began to cry. He held her close and rubbed her back. "I know this life is hard," he whispered in her ear. "I know what you've given up."

"It isn't giving up," Carrie said. "It's having you."

"There's still a lot to give up." He cupped her chin and kissed her. "But the life we lead is a lot less lonely when you have someone to share forever with."

"Yeah," Carrie agreed. "It is." And anything was better than being lonely—no matter what was lost.

———

Carrie remembered crying with Cody as she walked home from the hospital. She also continued to think about the possibilities Marliese had given her in tablet form.

When she thought of becoming like Cody, she'd taken time to consider what she'd miss when she was no longer human. She'd taken the time to deliberate her choice. She hadn't plunged into an undead life with Cody. It was simply that whenever the thought of aging, then dying, then leaving Cody behind entered her mind, she responded with a shudder and a deep, aching sadness.

She felt that sadness again when she imagined taking the pills Marliese had given her. The feeling made her pause her steps. It was a sadness she hadn't felt all night, even when she considered whether or not she wanted to be with Cody. But earlier that night, she thought she didn't have an option. It was either to live her life as a lonely vampire, or remain lonely with Cody. Perhaps with humanity at her fingertips, she could truly consider whether or not she wanted to stay the way she was so she could be with him.

Carrie soon reached their house. She walked inside and saw a clean kitchen floor. The TV was on, but this time, Cody turned to face her when she heard her.

"Hi," Carrie said as he stood up.

"I'm so sorry," Cody said as he walked towards her.

"You don't need to apologize—"

"I should've been more considerate before. I'm sorry."

"It's okay. I'm sorry too."

Cody pulled her close and kissed her hair. Though her skin no longer pulsed against his touch, she felt a warmth travel through her all the same. It was one unique to Cody's touch.

"I love you," Carrie said; and she meant it. That memory of Cody's touch, the sensation of Cody's love, was enough to keep her going. It was enough for her to stay. It was enough— for now. And even if it was only for a while, she had other possibilities ahead of her if they stopped being enough for her. She had a way to keep herself afloat, to be enough with or without someone else.

"I love you too," Cody said as he kissed her temple. "Always."

She smiled, but only she knew it was sly. "Forever."

'TIS BETTER TO WANT

Lydia had misbehaved before, but it was her seventh Christmas that brought the demon to her window.

One evening, about three weeks before Christmas, she got it in her head to steal some money from her mother's purse. She'd asked Santa for an American Girl doll and asked her family for other presents, but she wanted to buy something for herself. Her mother told her no, that she'd have plenty of presents on Christmas and didn't need another toy.

For Lydia, though, it was less about the toy itself and more about being able to buy it. She wanted to want something and be able to have it without asking permission. In order to do that, she needed some money.

Lydia waited until her mother tucked her in, then after fifteen minutes or so, tiptoed past the living room. The blue glow of the television told her she wouldn't be detected. Even so, she walked down the carpeted stairs one step at a time to ensure no creaks would bring her mother downstairs behind her.

Once downstairs, she walked to the wall where her mother's purse hung on a hook. She took it down, unzipped it, and saw her mother's purple beaded wallet shimmer up at her from the purse's depths.

A flicker in the window caught her eye. Lydia looked up, even though she figured it was her neighbor turning on their porchlight.

Two golden eyes stared at her through the glass. Lydia let out a yelp, then clamped her mouth shut. She looked at the stairs and listened for sounds of her mother coming downstairs.

She only heard the faint din of her mother's TV show. Lydia sighed—quietly—then turned to face the window again.

The golden eyes still looked at her. She saw that they belonged to a crimson face, a face that accentuated the shadows cast in the moonlight thanks to strong cheekbones and a cleft chin. The light from her neighbors' porch reflected off of black shapes coming from his head. They looked like horns.

He stared at Lydia, then raised a hand. His palm and fingers were also crimson, and his fingernails were long and black. He moved his pointer finger back-and-forth, like a clock, in a motion Lydia recognized as saying, "Ah ah ah," or, don't do that.

Though he didn't say what, Lydia felt in her bones that he meant she shouldn't steal. She placed the purse back on the hook, then immediately looked back at the demon. She felt hypnotized by his monstrosity. In a way, he was almost enchanting, like a magic creature in a fairy tale.

He nodded once, then turned and disappeared. Lydia stared out the window, seeing his stare long after he'd left.

———

Lydia didn't try to steal money from her mother again. She saw the demon's wagging finger in her mind throughout the following weeks, but she wasn't afraid of drawing his ire. Rather, she felt a need to make him happy, to ensure her part of the bargain between them.

Lydia found other ways to clash with her mother, though. It seemed with every inch she grew, they lost another ounce of patience with each other. As a teenager, Lydia grew more parched for independence, to do what she wanted to do. She wanted to stay out late without having to call home first, wanted to date that boy even though he was a senior, wanted just one glass of wine with dinner like the ones her mother enjoyed. But her mother seemed to only be able to say no, determined to have her remain a child who needed permission to do anything.

Rather than constantly ask, Lydia turned inward and kept her wants to herself, the one person who seemed to tell herself yes. Lydia cherished her time alone, and later, her time with friends. She stayed at their houses as often as possible. She found her home to be a constraint, one she wanted to break away from.

When she was seventeen, about the only thing Lydia liked about her mother was their resemblance to one another. After her mother would go to bed, Lydia would often sneak her mother's driver's license out of her purse and use it as a fake ID to get into clubs with her friends.

One night, about three weeks before Christmas, Lydia felt less excitement dancing and drinking with her friends. The blur of lights, jewelry, music, and grabby men left her cold. Still, it was better than being at home, and she drank in hopes of catching that feeling of freedom she'd had the other times she and her friends had been let in.

The only feeling she gained was nausea. After one too many, Lydia held her stomach and stumbled outside. She turned into the alleyway next to the club, thankfully devoid of smokers or other loiterers, and vomited into a trash can filled with the stench of crushed cigarettes and stale beer. Lydia crouched to the ground, and the cobblestones dug into her knees. She held her stomach and tried to calm her breathing.

"Seems you've had better nights than this one."

Lydia rolled her eyes, assuming one of the men in the club had followed her out. When she glanced in the direction of the voice, though, her eyes fell on a scarlet calf. The muscle curved and dipped its way into the rest of the leg, which was covered in brown fur that ended at the knee. Lydia's eyes moved slowly up the rest of his body, which was covered with the same brown fur until the neck and clavicle. Scarlet shoulders and the beginning of a scarlet chest peeked from a v-shape in the fur. Long black hair rested on the shoulders and against the neck. He looked down at her with a bemused smile.

He wasn't a man, though. He couldn't be, not with that scarlet skin and the onyx horns that protruded from his forehead. But Lydia wasn't afraid, especially when she saw his eyes. They were as deep and golden as she remembered, and the memories came flooding back to her through her sickened haze.

"It's you," she said as she got to her feet.

The demon furrowed his brow. "We've met?"

"Yeah, when I was seven," she said. It was Lydia's turn to be confused. Why was he here if he didn't remember her?

"You were looking in the window when I was about to steal some money from my mom."

The demon shrugged, and Lydia felt a twinge of offense. She hadn't thought of him that much, but she at least remembered him. Why didn't he remember her?

"I punish thousands of children every year," he said. "I don't remember all of you."

"Punish?"

"Yes. Just for a night." The demon held up a burlap sack and a tattered broom. "Santa gives gifts to the good children, but before Christmas, I visit the naughty ones. People say I steal them or eat them or other nonsense, but I only make them experience terror in my castle. They think it's a nightmare when they wake up the next morning—and the older they are when I punish them, the more terrifying their nightmares are."

"How terrifying?" Lydia asked.

The demon smiled at her, and his own eyes matched the flame in hers. "Surely you remember the worst nightmare you've ever had," he said in a low timbre that seemed to slink across the cobblestones and vibrate through Lydia's body. "One that makes you lie frozen in your bed, your heart still beating as if you've been running away from it, your skin clammy and your mind forever stamped with terrible images you'll never forget."

Lydia remembered her most terrifying nightmare. She'd had it when she was eight, and remembered it as clearly as she had when she woke up from it.

"That's what I give them," the demon said. "That's what I gave you."

"You didn't," Lydia said.

The demon's smile fell. Lydia clarified, "I saw you when I was awake. You told me not to steal—well, you wagged your finger at me—and then you disappeared."

"Hmm." The demon looked confused, but mostly embarrassed. "Well, I'm not entirely devoid of mercy."

"If you don't remember me, then why are you here?"

The demon regained his composure. "I'm rounding up the children who've been bad."

"So you're not here for me?"

The demon's face turned mischievous again. "Perhaps I am."

Lydia frowned. "I'm not a child, though."

"You're young enough to lie about how old you are." The demon nodded towards the club, and Lydia flushed with both anger and embarrassment.

"But I'm old enough to not be punished like some brat on the naughty list. What's your deal, anyway? You lurk around and scare kids who make a mistake?"

"Mistakes are mistakes. I don't punish children who misstep. I scare the ones whose naughtiness is deep within their souls, and will seep into something worse for everyone around them if I don't interfere." He hoisted his bag over his shoulder. "I'm not here for you, Lydia. You've made mistakes, but you're not bad."

Lydia felt a strange sadness at hearing him say he hadn't come for her.

"Are you sure about that?" she asked. A hint of flirtation tinged her voice.

If the demon heard it, he ignored it. "Yes. You want things, and sometimes you take less scrupulous routes to get them all the faster; but that isn't bad. It isn't a bad thing to want. Just be careful how you go about getting it."

Before she could respond, the demon waved, then disappeared around the corner. Lydia ran after him, but when she looked down the street, he was nowhere to be seen.

————

Back at home, Lydia couldn't sleep. Her mind kept wandering to the demon, the way he'd looked at her. How he'd teased her and spoken mischievously. The depth of his voice echoed in her ears, and his golden gaze stared back at her from her memories.

She turned onto her side and closed her eyes, sighing as she felt an ache in her soul for the demon to return.

Lydia crossed her thighs and squeezed in slow, repetitive motions. She imagined the demon staying with her in the alley, dropping his bag and pulling her close with both hands. She placed her hand between her thighs and added her fingers to the pulsing, her hand and hips moving in rhythm with her heart as her skin began to flush. Her thighs clenched, her cheeks burned, and when she felt her pleasure reach its highest point, she ceased moving and let out a cry.

Her body became awash in warm tingles as all of her muscles opened. She sighed and moaned into satisfied stillness. She glanced at her window, a part of her hoping that he would appear.

Lydia's window was empty. Still, she smiled as she stretched across her bed and felt her body cool. He'd told her to be careful about how she got the things she wanted. How could she be careful about getting him?

————

Lydia couldn't shake the demon from her mind. She saw his golden eyes and scarlet body wherever she went, heard his rolling voice in her ears no matter what noises surrounded her. She longed to see him again, to learn more about him and see what he wanted apart from doing his job. The demon had returned to her once. She had a feeling he'd be back.

In the meantime, she focused on her other wants. She did well in school—the demon was a tempter, but not enough of one to have her risk flunking out of high school and losing her chance to escape to college. She spent as much time as she wanted away from home. She still snuck into clubs, though with a greater sense of control over her actions (namely her drinking); and she felt the stirrings of lust for the boys in her presence. She made out with them in their cars and had sex with them in their rooms. They gratified her desires, or at least in lieu of that, gave her practice for the one she wanted most.

As she fucked a classmate named Ryan, she looked out his window and saw the blinking multicolored lights on his neighbor's porch. She wondered if the demon would pass through. She wondered if he would see her.

The street remained empty. "Come here," Ryan whispered as he placed a hand on the small of Lydia's back.

Lydia resisted, and Ryan paused from thrusting. "What's outside?" he asked.

"Nothing." Lydia lowered herself over Ryan and kissed him, hoping he hadn't noticed the sigh of disappointment that had come with her answer.

———

Lydia began to give up hope of ever seeing the demon again, even as her fantasies of him still flickered in her mind before she went to sleep. When she went away to college, she wondered briefly if the demon would come to her childhood home, looking for her.

It wasn't enough to make her go to her mother's. Instead, she spent the end of final exams sitting on the porch of her group home, smoking a cigarette as she clutched her jacket and looked at the stars. It was about three weeks until Christmas, but already, it was the best holiday she'd had in years. She was doing what she wanted to do, without restriction.

A shadow moved in her peripheral vision. She looked to the side, and her curiosity became delight. She saw a flash of crimson disappear behind the trees.

"Wait!" she called. Her voice rang down the street. She hoped that neither the neighbors nor her roommates heard her. She didn't want anyone to come outside and scare the demon away.

The trees remained still. Lydia stubbed out her cigarette and rushed down the street, ignoring the icy cold of the pavement beneath her slippered feet. "Wait!" she called again as she entered the copse of trees that separated her street from the next. She ran and ran, until she saw a shadow appear in the streetlight.

"Stop!" she said as she slowed her run. She didn't want to collide with the demon—not in the woods in the cold, anyway. "Please."

The demon turned and glared at her. "What do you want?" he asked.

"I wanted to see you again," Lydia said as she caught her breath.

"We've met?"

Lydia was less surprised than before that he didn't recognize her. If anything, she was glad. She'd been a girl both times before. She wanted him to see her and to know her as a woman.

"In passing," she said. "You've never punished me —"

The demon smiled. "Should I have?"

Lydia smiled back. She reached for him and held his elbow. He tensed beneath her, and his smile fell; but he didn't move his arm.

"Not then," Lydia said in a lower voice, one that had charmed many boys before. "I'd rather have you now."

The demon looked into her eyes. She wondered if he was trying to remember her. She hoped he was considering her.

She decided to aid his consideration. "I've thought about you ever since we met," she said as she traced her fingers down his forearm to his hand. "I've wanted you ever since we spoke."

"Lydia …"

She looked up at him as she held his hand. "You remember me?"

"In flickers. Human names come to me when I see them. I only know your name."

"You could know more." Lydia lifted his hand and placed it on her breast. Her heart picked up speed as she felt the heat of his palm on her skin. He breathed in, and his eyes broke away from hers to glance below her neck. She didn't mind. She loved it. She wanted him to want her.

The demon looked back up at her and into her eyes. His golden irises shone in the faint glow of the streetlight. Lydia felt so warm that her breath in the light could've been smoke.

He removed his hand from her breast. "I'm not here to satisfy desires," he said. "I'm here to punish."

"Then punish me," Lydia said. She reached for his hand, but he pulled it away.

"I don't punish those who ask. That's not my job."

"Is that all you're here for? Your job?"

"It is for the present."

Lydia felt her hopes crash into her stomach. "Then I'll leave you to it," she said. She turned and sped out of the woods, hoping the demon wouldn't follow her. She didn't want him to see her at her lowest.

————

Back at home, she lay in bed, unable to sleep. Her emotions clamored inside her like birds at war, with shame, sadness, and sexual frustration all clamoring for her heart's attention. None could claim it as fully as the memory of the demon.

Lydia wanted nothing more than to dash the demon from her brain, but the harder she tried, the more clearly she saw his face. She remembered the warmth of his skin to her touch, the glow of his eyes as he'd taken her in. He'd rejected her. He didn't want her. And yet she couldn't think of him with any sort of malice. She only thought of lost opportunities, of desires left unsatisfied.

When she finally slept, her rest was fitful. She spent most of the next day in a funk, unable to enjoy being done with classes for the semester. After dinner and Netflix with her roommates, she went to bed early.

She still couldn't sleep. She lay in bed, closed her eyes, and immediately saw the demon in her mind's eye.

"Lydia."

Lydia buried her head in her pillow and tried not to groan. Her stupid desires were so strong that she could even hear his voice.

"Lydia." A warm, familiar touch grazed her upper arm. She opened her eyes, looked up, and saw the demon standing over her.

Lydia screamed, and the demon jumped back.

"What the fuck!" she shouted.

"I didn't mean to frighten you —"

"How did you get in here?"

"I came in."

"What, like through the door?"

"Just through your room. I thought I was invited."

"You scared the shit out of me!"

"If you'd please calm down —"

"You don't fucking break into my room and then tell me to calm down!"

"I'm sorry! Stop shouting, please!"

Lydia sat up in bed and crossed her arms. "Pretty funny, a demon begging me for mercy."

The demon crossed his own arms and leaned against the wall. "About as funny as a human woman throwing herself at me in the woods in her pajamas."

Lydia flushed, and she hoped it was too dark for the demon to see her cheeks. "Why are you here if you don't want me?"

"I never said I didn't want you."

Lydia felt herself soften despite her best efforts. "You said you weren't here for my desires."

"I wasn't then. I couldn't. I had my job to do."

"So, wait, you're coming by the day after your shift? Why didn't you come yesterday?"

"I have to do what I come to Earth for. If I don't, there are consequences."

"What, the main devil will fire you?"

"Do you want to discuss the intricacies of Hell, or do you want to …" The demon faltered, and Lydia softened further at the sight of him growing embarrassed. It made her feel less like a rejected little girl, and more like she was speaking with someone who wanted to put his best foot forward—albeit awkwardly.

Lydia got out of bed and walked towards the demon. He straightened, but stayed put, even when she stopped a mere inch away from him.

"I can't stay on Earth for anything other than a set intention," the demon explained. "And I can't stay longer than that, or else I turn to ash. It was one of the rules put in place to ensure there wouldn't be another rebellion like Lucifer's. We do our errand, then leave."

"Then how come you're still here?"

"I came back today with a different purpose." He cupped her cheek, and Lydia trembled beneath his touch. "You."

Lydia tried not to sigh. She didn't want to seem weak to him, even though her body wanted nothing more than to fall into his arms.

"Do you still want me?" he asked.

Lydia looked into his eyes. Every desire she'd felt since she first wanted him swam to the surface of her skin.

"Yes," she said. "But …"

The demon arched an eyebrow, and Lydia gave him a small smile.

"First, I want you to punish me."

———

The journey to the demon's castle moved in flickers. The demon pulled her close, and Lydia leaned against his chest. In one moment, she felt warm rock beneath her feet. As soon as she looked up and caught a glimpse of fire all around her, she and the demon moved elsewhere, with warm rock replaced by cool slate. The walls around her matched the floors, grey and shiny beneath the lights.

"I'm surprised you don't have torches," Lydia said as she tapped a lightbulb hanging from the ceiling like a pendulum.

"Hell isn't so torturous that we can't have electricity," the demon said.

Lydia looked around the room. It was mostly bare, save for a black cupboard, the demon's burlap sack, and a broom. "Is this where you take the people you punish?" she asked.

"Yes, but they don't usually see it. They stay in here—" the demon lifted the bag—"and hang from there."

He pointed above her head. Lydia looked up and saw a mammoth-sized hook hanging from the ceiling.

"So ... do I need to go in there?" Lydia asked as she looked at the bag.

"You're quite obsessed with being punished. Why is that?"

Lydia felt she owed him honesty, but all the same, she reddened. "It's what you said you do to people," she said. "And I want to experience you the way those lucky enough to be captured by you have."

The demon kept his smirk, but Lydia saw his eyes soften. "They wouldn't think themselves lucky."

"They're not me."

"And I won't treat you like them."

Before Lydia could protest, her arms whipped over her head. The motion yanked her upward, just enough to put her on tiptoe. She felt satin wrap around her wrists and fasten her to the hook.

Lydia smiled as the demon moved closer to her. "I'm not treating you as my task," he said. "I'm treating you as my lover."

"Have you had lovers before?"

The demon gave her a look that asked if she was serious, and Lydia chuckled in spite of herself. "I'm centuries old, Lydia. I've had many women and men in my room." He drew his finger across her chin. "But here and now, I'm with you." His finger moved down her neck and between her breasts. Lydia closed her eyes and sighed. "And I'm generous to those I'm with."

She felt his hand move down her waist. She realized she could feel his palm upon her bare skin. She opened her eyes, looked down, and saw that she was naked. Her pajamas lay in a heap against the cupboard.

The demon cupped her breast and kissed her neck. Lydia closed her eyes again, not caring how she'd lost her clothes. All she cared about was being close to him. All she cared about was getting what she wanted, what she'd wanted for so long.

"And part of that generosity," he whispered in her ear, "is giving you what you want." He let her go and moved towards the broom.

"What do you use the broom for?" Lydia asked, though she had an inkling.

"It aids in the generation of fears. I swat the punished with this to brush their nightmares across their minds. Their thoughts move in panicked swirls, clouding what they think is real or fake—all while in the darkness of the sack."

"Pretty intricate."

129

"We don't half-ass in Hell." The demon smiled as he moved past the broom. "But the broom is for —"

"Your tasks and not for me, right?" Lydia hoped she didn't sound too disappointed.

"Right." He opened the cupboard and reached inside. He turned to face her, and Lydia's disappointment quickly vanished.

"This is for you," the demon said, as he snapped the whip he held in both hands. "I think you'll find it much more gratifying."

———

The first lash caused Lydia to cry out in shock. It quickly melted into delight. The stinging bubbled into a warm throbbing that vibrated like a heartbeat across her skin. The demon whipped her again, and her cry was one of pleasure.

"Do you know what you've done?" the demon asked.

Lydia opened her eyes and furrowed her brow. "What?"

The whip cracked across her back. She bit her lip, relishing the sensation.

"Do you know why I've brought you here?" The demon circled in front of her, the whip's tail dragging behind him. "Why you're receiving this punishment?"

Lydia was about to ask him why he wanted to know when he obviously knew, until he arched his eyebrow. Lydia then understood: he wanted her to play the part. "Because I need to be punished," she said.

"For what?"

"For what I've done."

"Tell me the things you've done." He cracked the whip against her legs, and Lydia sighed.

"You don't give me much of a reason to spill when you whip me anyway," she teased.

The demon's mouth stayed set, but she saw a smile glimmer in his eyes. He rolled the whip into his palm. "What have you done?" he asked.

"I …" Lydia tried to think of anything but sex, but it was proving difficult. "I lied to my professor. I said I was sick, but I was making a pot run with my roommate."

The demon flicked her lightly with the tip of the whip. "Hardly worth the punishment I'm capable of."

Lydia pressed her lips as the demon chuckled to himself. "I drank underage," she said. He gave her a smarter lash, and she smiled. "I did it almost all the time. I broke into my mother's liquor cabinet once and downed half a bottle of Four Roses with my friend Patti. We both threw up in the woods."

"Wasn't throwing up punishment enough?"

"No. I need a different kind of pain."

The demon complied. He whipped the sides of her legs, then her hips. Lydia groaned and arched her back as the stinging traveled up her body.

"I lied to my mother all the time. I didn't want to live with her. I'd stay over with boys and tell them I cared about them if it meant I could stay at their house."

The whip smacked across her butt. "You did this often?"

"Yes." Another lash across her butt. Lydia felt a wave of sensations between her legs. She clenched her thighs together to relish the feeling. She remembered feeling that way when she first felt lust for the demon. Now, he was with her. Now, she could have him. "I fucked them and made them think they wanted me," she said. "When all this time, I wanted you."

The whip lashed across her shoulder blades. "You lied to them."

"And lusted for you. I've never wanted anyone as much as you. I wanted you so much that when I saw you yesterday, I had to follow you and I had to have you. I'm so consumed with lust, I feel like I'm going to burst."

Lydia clenched her body in anticipation of the lashing. None came. Lydia opened her eyes, then saw the demon walk back in front of her. He set the whip on the ground.

"I won't punish you for lust," he said.

"Isn't it a sin?" she asked as she licked her lips.

The demon breathed in, his golden eyes aflame. Lydia looked down to see if he felt as aroused as she did. She saw nothing but fur, and wondered briefly if his cock was also fur.

The demon's arms obstructed her view. His hands dipped under the fur at his waist, and he lifted it like a shirt. He pulled the top over his head to reveal a scarlet, muscled chest. Lydia's mouth dropped a little as she took in the curves of his body.

"It isn't a sin to want," he said. "I don't consider it so, anyway. Especially when a beautiful woman is the one doing the wanting."

"Especially when she wants you?" Lydia breathed.

The demon gave a small smile. "It helps." He moved towards her, then hooked his thumbs into the fur around his waist. "But either way, it isn't something I punish. Desires aren't meant to be punished." He removed his pants and revealed a hardened cock, the sight of which sent a sudden rush between Lydia's thighs. "Desires are meant to be satisfied."

The demon held her waist, and the satin ribbon around her wrists became undone. She wrapped her arms around his shoulders and pressed herself against his erection.

"Satisfy them for me," she whispered.

————

In a fleeting moment, they were in the demon's room. There were stone walls and a bed with fur blankets. A single lamp hung from the ceiling, giving the room's occupants just enough light to see each other.

Lydia barely paid the room any notice. She gripped the demon as hard as he gripped her, both of them kissing the other with increasing fervor. Lydia ran her palms along his back, his ass, his waist and his neck. She traced her fingers up to his horns. They were rippled and felt like polished stone.

The demon spun her towards his bed and lowered her to the mattress. She sighed upon the touch of the fur blankets against her skin, warm and soft, and smooth as silk. The demon released her, then lowered himself over her to lay her flat upon the bed. He kissed her eyes, her mouth, her ears, and her neck. He gripped her breasts, his thumb running circles over her erect nipples. He took her breast and began to suck; Lydia arched her back and moaned.

His kisses left her breast and continued down her stomach. Lydia opened her legs. Her inner thighs were already moist from the rushes she'd experienced during her punishment.

The demon opened her legs further and lowered his head. He looked up at her, smiled, then moved in closer. His tongue stroked her clit, then plunged inside of her.

Lydia gasped, then moaned as she felt his tongue go deeper with every stroke. It seemed with every lick the demon gave, his tongue went in further and further. Lydia cried out, her body tensing and beginning to sway.

The demon lifted his head from between her thighs. His tongue remained out, and Lydia saw it hanging below his chin before he closed his mouth. She marveled at the size of it—though from what she'd seen before, it was only the second biggest thing of his that she'd have inside of her.

The demon wiped his chin and moved back up to her face. Before he could lower himself over her, Lydia rose to greet him. She curled her arm around his shoulders and, as she began to kiss him, turned him over. She lowered him to the bed and crawled on top of him.

The demon held her by the waist and took her in, his eyes ravenous. Lydia began to thrust overtop of him, moving her hips as she leaned back and rubbed her hands over her breasts. She then thrust herself forward, her hair brushing across his chest as she kissed him. He held her close as she kissed him all over his upper body. She kissed and sucked his nipples, bit his neck more and more with every sigh of pleasure she heard escape from his lips.

The demon's cock throbbed beneath her. Lydia ached with wanting between her thighs. It was time. She slid off of him and got onto her hands and knees.

The demon grinned as he held her ass, then entered her from behind. Lydia cried out in ecstasy, the first touch of him to her creating a heat that only grew with every thrust. The demon smacked her ass, and Lydia cried out again. She tried to slow her thrusting so that this moment she'd craved for so long would last.

The demon slid out of her, then turned her over onto her back. "I want to see you," he said as he pulled her to him by her ankles. He lowered himself between her. Lydia held his cock and guided him back into her. He moaned and she sighed upon his cock reentering her. He began to thrust, and Lydia wrapped her legs around his waist. She gripped him by the shoulders and scratched his back, her nails moving up and down in slow, lingering trails.

His thrusts grew faster, his breathing more labored. Lydia knew he was close, and so was she. His cock pressed and pressed, and she throbbed around him as he thrust. Her body tensed and her skin became awash in tingles.

The demon arched his back and cried out. His pumping slowed as he came, and Lydia felt her body tighten further, her cries becoming shortened around the orgasm swelling within. As the demon finished and withdrew, Lydia let out a rippling moan as every sensation she'd felt for the demon coursed through her body. She lay against the blankets, curling her body as it came down from immense satisfaction. The demon lowered himself to her side and held her close. She turned and lay against his chest, both of them breathing in time with the other.

———

Lydia fell asleep easily in the demon's arms. It seemed she'd barely been in the fog of sweet dreams, though, when he shook her awake.

"Lydia," the demon whispered, though with a sense of urgency.

"Is something wrong?" she murmured. She felt too warm, and kicked off the blanket.

"Not yet. But you cannot sleep here."

Lydia chuckled a little. "I should've guessed a demon wouldn't let me stay the night afterward."

"It's not that. Believe me, I'd like nothing more."

She saw that the demon didn't share her smile, and decided to keep her jokes to herself.

"But you can't stay here—not for long. The rules that apply to me on Earth apply to living humans in Hell. If you stay too long, you'll burn."

Lydia noticed her body still felt warm, even with the blanket tossed aside. Beads of sweat pricked her forehead. "Can I come back?" she asked.

"Only if I bring you back."

"Will you bring me back?"

The demon held her cheek, and Lydia felt her heart grow heavy. "I won't be able to right away," he said. "Nor nightly. But I will want you again, and if you still want me as well, then yes, I will."

Lydia smiled, then looked down when she suddenly felt cool cotton upon her thighs. Her pajamas rested in her lap. "How do you do that?" she asked.

"I was born with the ability."

Lydia thought of returning to her bed and her home, alone, without the demon's golden eyes to stare into when she woke up. She understood she couldn't stay. Still, though, the wanting that she had for him bubbled in her heart. She wondered if it would ever dissipate. She hoped it never would.

She cupped his cheek and kissed him. "Come back whenever you can," she said. "I'll definitely want you."

The demon smiled, then kissed her back.

"But next time you do," she added, "maybe give me a warning before waking me up in my room."

————

Lydia remembered one last kiss, then nothing else which brought her back to her bed. She awoke beneath her own blanket as the morning sun crept through the window.

Part of her wondered, with a bit of fear, if she had only dreamed of her night with the demon. The wonder didn't last long. She noticed she was naked beneath her sheets. Her pajamas were folded neatly on her bedside table. She got out of bed, walked to her full-length mirror, and turned around. She saw welts from the lashes he'd given her all across her back.

Lydia smiled.

————

December passed, and one year became another. Lydia didn't see the demon. She focused on school, a summer job, her friends. She saw other men, though the thought of the demon returning kept her from getting too close.

The demon, however, didn't come. As summer became fall, she wondered if he would ever return. She believed that he wanted her, but he lived in Hell, after all. Hell wasn't built for their pleasures.

As fall lingered on, though, and her time away from him grew longer, she felt desire for him grow. Her thoughts began to cloud with memories of his hands and his tongue. She'd imagine the whip across her back and have to cross her legs beneath her desk. She imagined lying beside him and feeling him breathe next to her. She'd fall asleep at night and dream of him.

One evening, about three weeks before Christmas, Lydia went downstairs to get a cup of tea after her roommates had all gone to sleep. She walked to the cupboard and reached for a mug.

Her hand paused midair when she glanced at the window. She saw two golden eyes staring back at her.

She faced the window with a smile.

The demon smiled back, but didn't say a word. He simply raised his hand, then beckoned her with his finger.

A Note From the Author

Thanks for reading *Someone to Share My Nightmares: Stories*! If you could please take a minute to review the book on Amazon or Goodreads, I'd really appreciate it.

Acknowledgments

My editor, Evelyn Duffy, and I have a running joke about how she'll almost always suggest I add another sex scene to my stories. For this collection, she referred to her tendency to do this as reliable as *Groundhog Day*. Because yes, even though I wrote a collection where almost every story has sex in it, she advised me to add another one to one of the stories.

We laugh about it because of the consistency, but also because of how funny it is that my editor would ask me to add more sex. Sex scenes are often seen as extemporaneous in literature. Stories that include it are seen as porn, exploitative, or part of the oft-derided romance genre. I find this a little sad. Sex is a part of many of our lives. As V. Castro said in her foreword to this book, it's natural and normal.

Yet as far as we've come as a culture, we still take a puritanical approach to sex. Earlier this year, I wrote a guest post for Divination Hollow (www.divinationhollow.com) about sex in horror. Usually when sex is in a horror story, it's either a way to see who'll get killed first in a slasher film, or wildly gross and juvenile. Tender moments exist, but a genre otherwise obsessed with pushing boundaries and not being shy is actually quite shy about good, romantic, consensual sex.

Someone to Share My Nightmares is not my first foray into sexy horror. It appears as early as my first collection, *The Crow's Gift and Other Tales*, in "All the Pieces Coming Together." But with this collection, I wanted to be more deliberate about creating a theme of love and sex interwoven with horror. I found it interesting to see how the terror changed when two people (and their libidos) were involved as opposed to one person. Having sex, and even being in love, is a willingness to place yourself into vulnerability. I think horror does well when it explores that idea further.

I'm grateful for the opportunity to explore these themes in my writing. Much of that opportunity has come from Evelyn Duffy's encouragement. Evelyn has been my editor from the beginning, and I always find her insight to be invaluable. I appreciate her edits and suggestions that helped me shape this collection.

I also want to thank V. Castro for writing the foreword, for allowing me the opportunity to co-manage Fright Girl Summer with her, and for being a wonderful writing peer and friend. I love her work, and I highly encourage you all to read her books!

Many thanks to Doug Puller for an amazing cover, title page illustration, and for formatting the book. I miss working next to you in an office, but I'm glad we can keep in touch through our projects and annual Christmas cards.

Thanks to my parents for always encouraging my writing career, even when I'm writing stuff like this collection that may make them uncomfortable to read it. Your support means the world to me.

Finally, I want to thank my husband, Will; who is my biggest cheerleader and who always makes me feel loved.

Previously Published Works

"The Parrot" was previously published in a slightly different form in *We Are Wolves*, eds. Gemma Amor and Laurel Hightower; from Burial Day Press.

"Petal, Page, Piel" was previously published in a slightly different form in *The Sirens Call*, Issue 46: "Summer Nightscares."

Content Warnings

The following is a list of content/trigger warnings for this collection. They may be considered spoilers for their respective stories.

Someone to Share My Nightmares, Bump in the Night, The Parrot, The Sharps, You Promised Me Forever: sex (detailed but not explicit or pornographic)

Petal Page Piel: skinning/flaying (alluded to but not shown)

The Parrot: domestic abuse, mental abuse, physical abuse (discussed but not shown), strangling

Candy: beating/bludgeoning

Bump in the Night, The Sharps, Your Promised Me Forever: blood (heavy focus as opposed to a brief mention)

'Tis Better to Want: whipping/BDSM (consensual), explicit sexual content

Photo by Karen Papadales

About the Author

Sonora Taylor is the author of several short stories and novels, including *Seeing Things, Little Paranoias: Stories,* and *Without Condition.* In 2020, she won the Ladies of Horror Fiction awards for Best Collection (*Little Paranoias*) and Best Novel (*Without Condition*). Her short stories have been published by Camden Park Press, Burial Day Press, Kandisha Press, Cemetery Gates Media, Sirens Call Publications, Tales to Terrify, and others.

Along with V. Castro, Sonora co-manages Fright Girl Summer (frightgirlsummer.com), an online book festival promoting marginalized authors and voices. In 2022, Sonora and Nico Bell will edit an anthology of fat-positive horror called *Diet Riot: A Fatterpunk Anthology.*

Sonora is currently working on her fourth novel. She lives in Arlington, Virginia, with her husband and a rescue dog.

Visit Sonora online at sonorawrites.com.

Made in the USA
Monee, IL
21 October 2021